THE LAWYER

THE
RETRIBUTIONERS

as written by
WAYNE D. DUNDEE

AN EDWARD A. GRAINGER SERIES

ISBN: 978-1-943035-07-6

 BEAT to a PULP
PO Box 173
Freeville, New York 13068
USA
Email: btapzine@beattoapulp.com
Visit us at www.beattoapulp.com

CONTENTS

CHAPTER ONE

Dusk was just settling as The Lawyer rode into the northern Texas town of Emmett. The false-fronted buildings lining the main drag cast long, oddly-shaped shadows, some of them converging in the middle of the street, poking at one another as if they were jousting atop the dusty wagon ruts.

After stabling his Morgan mare, Redemption, at what looked to be a well-appointed livery and arranging for her to be fed top quality hay and an extra scoop of grain, The Lawyer headed across the street toward a large building marked with a prominent sign identifying it as a hotel. To anyone taking notice, he was a middle-aged man of average height, trim and solid-looking, clad in trail clothes that, although dusty and a bit worn, were of good cut and quality. He carried his saddlebags slung over his left shoulder and a possibles pack was gripped in his left hand. To the trained eye, it would be evident this was designed to leave his right hand unencumbered for accessing, if need be, the big Remington revolver riding on his right hip in a hand-tooled leather holster.

As The Lawyer angled toward the hotel, his gazed

drifted farther up the street to a squat stone building near its end. There was a small sign fastened beside the building's heavy wooden front door. From this distance, in the descending murkiness, The Lawyer couldn't make out exactly what it said. But it didn't matter, really. The building was distinct enough to leave little doubt that it housed the town marshal's office and jail.

First thing tomorrow, his business would take him there. For tonight, however, The Lawyer's superseding priorities were for some good whiskey, a hearty meal, a bath, and some deep sleep in an actual bed rather than a bedroll beside a campfire. Nevertheless, his gaze continued to linger for an extra moment on the marshal's office/jail. As a result, he was actually looking directly at it when the back side suddenly erupted outward in a thundering, ear-pounding explosion!

The sound rolled up the street like the rush of a windstorm, rebounding off building fronts, rattling window glass, causing the ground to tremble. At this time of day, the street was nearly empty. Most of the businesses lining it were closed, patrons and proprietors gone home for supper. Only Emmett's two saloons were flourishing and, in a matter of seconds, curious heads were poking out of each.

"Holy shit! What just happened?"

"What the hell was that?"

Frozen in the middle of the street, The Lawyer had a sinking feeling that he knew the answer to those rhetorical questions. He'd already taken a step toward the ruptured building—a boiling cloud of dust rising up behind it and fragments of debris now starting to clatter back to earth after being hurled high and wide—when gunfire began popping from within and without, accompanied by angry shouts and excited whoops.

That's when The Lawyer knew for certain— *Jailbreak!*

Dropping the saddlebags and possibles pack as the Remington seemed to leap to his hand by its own volition, The Lawyer broke into a run straight for the heart of the noise and chaos.

At the same time, two men came half-staggering, half-running out the front door of the jail building. Both were wielding handguns and both were covered in a thick layer of grayish dust. One of the men stumbled and fell to his knees. The second man leaned over him and struggled to lift him to his feet. Before he could succeed, six horsemen burst out of the massive dust cloud billowing around from either end of the shattered building and came charging wildly toward the two men in the street.

The pair on foot—lawmen of some sort who'd been on duty inside, The Lawyer surmised—opened fire on the riders even as the star packer who'd fallen remained on his knees. But the riders were firing, too, throwing a hail of lead ahead of the surging bodies and pounding hooves of their mounts. The lawmen scarcely had a chance. Both of them were knocked flat, bullet-riddled and then trampled savagely as the fleeing horses were purposely reined to pass directly over them.

When the horsemen swung in his direction and came barreling down the street, The Lawyer veered sharply to his right and went into a diving roll that carried him scrambling for cover behind a water trough placed at one end of a hitch rail. As he skidded across the muddy ground immediately surrounding the base of the tank, bullets whacked and walloped the wooden encasement, kicking up mini-geysers of water and causing the thick, treated boards to shiver with each impact.

Twisting frantically, raising himself on his free elbow, The Lawyer squeezed off some rapid-fire return rounds as the riders drew even and then passed by his position. He had the satisfaction of seeing one of them pitch sideways out of his saddle. But, at almost the same instant, the side of his head just above his left ear flared with fierce pain, like a branding iron had been touched to it. He jerked away, his support elbow slipping in the mud, and fell momentarily onto the flat of his back.

At least he meant for it to be momentary. But when he tried to push himself back up, the inside of his head went into a dizzying spin and the arm he tried to push with seemed to have turned flabby and useless. He could only lay there, hearing the continued sounds of the gunshots and pounding hooves. Then came a great cacophony of breaking glass as the riders began indiscriminately shooting out the windows of the street-side shops and stores.

Finally, The Lawyer managed to pull himself up to a sitting position by grabbing the lip of the water trough. Over the rim, he saw a couple of the riders reining to slow their mounts up toward the end of town where he had ridden in only a short time ago, just across from the livery stable. They appeared to be arguing about something.

The Lawyer could hear part of the words: "What about Pedro? He went down back there!"

"Ain't nothing we can do for him now—We can't go back, we've got to hightail it!"

The matter was settled by the appearance of men pouring out of the two saloons located diagonally across the street from one another, both establishments having just gotten their front windows shot to hell by the fleeing horsemen. Their drinking so rudely inter-rupted by first the explosion and then the reckless gunfire, these gun-toting customers were in a foul mood and neither reluctant nor hesitant to show it. Spilling somewhat drunkenly out into the street, they formed two ragged lines facing the direction the horsemen had gone and opened up on the straggling riders. What they lacked in accuracy they tried to make up for in eagerness and the sheer volume of lead they poured in the direction of the jailbreakers. As far as The Lawyer could tell, they failed to score any meaningful hits but they sure as hell sent the lagging horsemen on their way with renewed vigor.

Whatever happened next, The Lawyer went blank on. When he tried to drag himself to a standing position, another head-spinning wave rolled over him and this time when he fell back he dropped deep into a pool of unconsciousness.

CHAPTER TWO

As soon as he came to, even before opening his eyes, The Lawyer felt the urge to try and sit up. But gentle words and strong hands pushing against his chest held him down.

"Take it easy, mister. You don't want to be moving around too sudden."

He got his eyes open. Narrowed slits under scowling brows. Looking around, he saw that he'd been lifted up onto a section of boardwalk not far from the water trough behind which he'd ducked for cover. By the degree of darkness thickening the shadows up and down the street, The Lawyer gauged he had been out for only a short time.

His head and shoulders were propped up on something—his own saddlebags, he realized after a moment. A knot of men were gathered around him, looking down anxiously. One of them, a youngish fellow with spectacles and an unruly spill of ginger hair, was kneeling beside him and still had a restraining hand resting on The Lawyer's chest.

"I'm a doctor," the bespectacled man said. "You're going to be fine, but if you try to get up too quickly it likely will cause some dizziness or nausea. Maybe both."

The Lawyer slowly raised his left hand to that side of his head. His fingers gently prodded a soft, lumpy bandage.

"You got grazed by a bullet," the doctor said. "Gave you a good smack, but didn't crack the skull or anything. Split some skin but your blood coagulates well. The bleeding was almost stopped by the time I got to you. I went ahead and put on a bandage in case it tries to leak some more when you start moving around. Probably should throw a couple of stitches through it when you feel strong enough to come over to my office."

The Lawyer said, "The two men in the street out front of the jail. The ones who got shot and then rode down?"

The doctor shook his head. "They weren't so lucky."

"The rider I shot?"

"Him neither. Not that anybody here is lamenting the loss."

One of the men hovering near said, "If you hadn't been on hand to help discourage his compadres by plugging that one the way you did, stranger, no tellin' how much more hell they would've raised before they rode on."

"I saw plenty of other men pouring out into the street and helping to put the run on those marauders," The Lawyer countered.

"Yeah, and I was one of 'em," the man said. "Only

trouble is, we failed at cuttin' down any more of the bastards. Damn the luck."

When the doctor thought it prudent, he helped The Lawyer sit up. When this produced no adverse reactions, the other man assisted in getting the patient to his feet and from there he and the doctor proceeded up the street and on into the next block where the medic's office awaited. Once there, as the goal of "throwing in" the aforementioned stitches got underway, the doctor (a shingle over his door identifying him as one Dr. T. Aarons, M.D.) proceeded to fill The Lawyer in on more of the details behind the fracas he'd flung himself into the middle of.

* * *

"Three days ago," Doc Aarons explained as The Lawyer tried to get his eyes accustomed to the brilliance of the lamps turned up so brightly in a pristine white treatment room, "the Emmett bank was honored by a visit from the Selkirk gang, led by brothers Ike and Owen. In case you're unfamiliar with the Selkirks, they're a rather notorious pack of outlaws who've branded their name deep and bloody all across northern Texas over the past couple years."

"Haven't been up this way all that long," said The Lawyer, skeptically eyeing the gleaming tip of a curved needle into whose eye Aarons was carefully inserting a slender thread. "But, yes, I've heard mention of the Selkirks."

"They raid down here, then flee north across the border to lay low in the Indian Nations until they're ready to pull the next job. Then they swoop down again. They hit sudden and savage and somehow manage to keep eluding our Texas Rangers down here, as well as the handful of U.S. Marshals spread way too thin trying to cover that cesspool of outlaws the 'Nations have become a haven for."

"You make them sound like a real troublesome bunch." The Lawyer paused to suck a quick intake of breath as the doctor's needle passed in and out of the split in the skin just above his ear. "How did Emmett get lucky enough to attract their attention?"

Before he could answer, the doctor had to pull in the tip of his tongue, which he'd thrust out one corner of his mouth while concentrating on the job at hand. "Luck, you say. Luck's a mighty peculiar thing, isn't it—the way it can whipsaw back and forth in an individual's life or over the course of things in general? You see, up until not so long ago, our little town and its bank likely wouldn't have had any appeal to the Selkirk gang. Wouldn't have presented a big enough haul. But then the cattle operations around here started getting bigger. And more businesses and people started moving in. And so the bank started having to keep more money on hand to cover the various transactions and one thing another." He kept right on talking as he pulled another stitch through The Lawyer's split skin. "Well, all of that seemed like a good thing. Good luck, right?"

"But then," The Lawyer ventured, trying to concentrate more on what Aarons was saying rather than on what he was doing, "bad luck reared its ugly head when all the new prosperity got big enough so it *did* have some appeal to the Selkirks."

"You got it. But here comes an example of how luck, like I said before, can whipsaw back the other way. The day before the gang was planning to hit—while they were camped north of town doing whatever last minute things it is an outlaw gang does at a time like that—a stubborn old prospector named Thornberry, who roams the hills up that way, spotted them. He was smart enough to stay out of sight because he thought right away there was something suspicious about a hard-looking bunch like that camped out there in the middle of nowhere. When Thornberry scouted them a little closer, he started seeing things that told him plain enough who they were and what they likely were up to."

"Things like what?"

"Well. For starters, he saw a woman in their midst. That would've been Lolena Tabor, a pretty notorious character in her own right."

"I've heard that name, too."

"She reportedly has been with the gang for quite a while. No beauty by any stretch—again, according to reports—but she apparently still knows how to keep a man interested. She supposedly switches back and forth between the two brothers. Honeys up with Ike for a while, until they get in a row; then goes with Owen until things blow up between them; then makes up with Ike again for a spell, and so on and so forth."

The Lawyer cocked the eyebrow on the opposite of his head from where Aarons was working. "You seem awfully well versed on the inner workings of this bunch."

The doc chuckled. "I guess I do, don't I? Believe me, it's not an obsession or anything. Until they showed up right here in our back yard, I knew only the basics. Probably not much more than you. But since they made their attempt on our bank, it's pretty much all anyone around here has been talking about. So I've gotten a thorough education on the Selkirk gang. More, I dare say, than I ever really wanted."

"You said they made an 'attempt' on your bank?"

"Oh, yes. They sure did. But forewarned by the report from Thornberry, the prospector, our marshal and his deputies were ready for them. Hell, practically the whole town was armed and ready. Once the gang had ridden in and started to close around the bank, the marshal—that would be Ed Maynard, one of the unfortunates who died this evening in the street out front of the jail—called out for them to throw down their guns and give it up, no one would get hurt."

"But, of course, they didn't comply."

Aarons heaved a forlorn sigh. "No. They didn't … Ironically, it was the woman—Lolena Tabor—who made their intentions to do otherwise plenty clear. I could hear her, plain as day, from where I was staying out of the way here inside my office. 'Eat shit and die, you Texas tinhorns!' she hollered. And then all hell broke loose. Guns began blazing all up and down the street, everybody was shouting and cussing, the gang members were riding wildly back and forth, trying to find a place to break out, ride free. Amazingly, they managed to pull off their escape. All but one."

12

"Ike Selkirk himself."

"You knew that?"

"I heard about it on my way here. Like you said, a lot of tongues are wagging since that attempted bank robbery."

Having ceased his stitching, Aarons took half a step and examined his work. Then, snapping a satisfied nod, he announced, "Yeah, that ought to do it. I doubt it will do any more bleeding but let me apply a small bandage over it, just in case."

"Whatever you think best."

"It'll provide some cushion, too, in case your hat tilts a little and rides there." The doc made a gesture to said hat, resting on The Lawyer's knee. "Speaking of which, that's a kind of interesting lid you've got there. Don't know that I've ever seen one quite like that before."

The head gear in question was rather distinct in design. It somewhat resembled a flat-crowned Stetson that was very common throughout the area. But the brim, though fairly wide, was not quite as broad as that of a Stetson. And the crown rose three to four inches higher.

"No, even though I myself have grown to like it, the design never really caught on," The Lawyer admitted. "It was the brainchild of a haberdasher friend of mind. The idea was that it would be suitable for everyday wear, as you see it now, or, for special occasions, it could be adjusted to a more formal look."

Demonstrating, he reached inside the hat, pressed a hidden button, and the crown rose another four inches to create what could be considered a serviceable top hat, though not quite a stovepipe.

"Well, I'll be," Aarons marveled. "That's about the doggonedest thing I ever saw. But it never caught on, you say?"

"Don't know that I've ever seen another like it."

"You know, that's kinda too bad. If there were any available, I believe I'd get one for myself. I surely would."

As he finished applying the bandage, the doc said, "Getting back to those wagging tongues, I guess mine has been doing a pretty good job of that, too, hasn't it?"

The Lawyer shrugged. "I thought it was part of your bedside manner—to distract me with what you were saying instead of the fact you were repeatedly poking a sharp object into me."

"Hadn't thought of it that way, but maybe you're onto something. Maybe it's a tactic I'll employ again in the future."

The Lawyer felt pretty sure that jabbering while he worked wasn't exactly a habit the young doctor had only just acquired. In any case, it had proved useful not only as a distraction from the needle but had also provided some worthwhile tidbits of information. Something The Lawyer was covertly very much in the market for.

"Since it sounds like your late marshal was a fairly savvy lawman," he prodded off-handedly, "I'm surprised he wasn't better prepared for the possibility— hell, you might even say *probability*—there'd be an attempt to spring Ike. Not only was he one of the gang's leaders but, on top of that, brother Owen surely would feel a blood obligation not to leave him behind and penned up."

"Oh, Marshal Maynard recognized that okay," Aarons affirmed. "He took plenty of steps to try and be prepared. Started by calling in the Rangers to get Ike hauled off and kept somewhere else, somewhere stronger and more secure than our little jail, while all the charges against him were being gathered and a trial arranged. Far as we know, some Rangers to escort him away should be showing up anytime. Although, no matter how soon they get here now, now it will unfortunately be too late.

"In the meantime, the marshal had also taken numerous other steps where guarding the prisoner was concerned. Two men stationed inside the jail, watching him round the clock. And additional deputized men stationed all the time at key points around the outside of town, ready to give warning at the first sign of anything or anybody that looked like the gang might be making a return."

The Lawyer nodded. "That's right. One of them stopped me on my way into town. Wonder how the gang made it around those fellas?"

"That's one of the big questions since the jailbreak," said the doctor, his expression turning sour. "One of our regular deputies rode out to make the circuit of watch points, check on the men. The fear is that we've probably got a lookout out there who was caught off guard. With any luck, he was only chunked on the head, maybe tied up. But, with the Selkirk gang, that's probably too much to hope for."

"Hate to give rats like that any credit," said The Lawyer thoughtfully. "But the way they timed that breakout was daring and pretty clever all the way around."

"How so?"

"Well. Think about it. You'd usually figure a thing like that to get tried in the wee hours ahead of daybreak. That's when and why men on guard duty *try* to be at their most alert. But it's nevertheless a natural lag time for the mind and body, meaning it's always a vulnerable period. So this bunch aimed to outfox the kind of thinking that might go into covering that vulnerable stretch and instead they hit at another, more unexpected lag period. … Suppertime."

Aarons eyed him a bit more closely than he had up until that point. "You some kind of former military man or something?"

A rare, brief smile touched The Lawyer's lips. "No. Not hardly. Just rolling some things around in my mind is all."

Any further discussion that might have occurred between the two men was held at bay by a surge of voices from outside and the sound of a horse galloping down the street.

"It's Deputy Tell, returning from checking on the outlying lookouts," the doc announced after a quick glance out the window.

CHAPTER THREE

It was two hours later before The Lawyer finally got settled in his hotel room. The establishment, like so many of the businesses up and down the street, had suffered its share of damage from the punishing spray of bullets thrown by the jailbreakers as they fled town. In the hotel's case, its front windows and part of the inside lobby were thoroughly riddled. This meant all members of the staff were frantically involved in the clean-up, leaving only limited attention available for a lone guest.

But a few well-placed bills in the right hands nevertheless got The Lawyer his room, a decent meal (although served in the kitchen), a bottle of top quality bourbon, and a promise from one of the maids that she would somehow make time to ensure his soiled clothes were cleaned and ready for him first thing in the morning. In the meantime, he donned fresh attire from the spare clothes in his saddlebags—after, that was, cleaning up and shaving at the room's wash basin since not even his charm and the offer of more bills were enough to wangle a hot bath in the midst of the damage control.

Still, the bed was comfortable, the room was relatively quiet, and The Lawyer was properly exhausted after a long day on the trail capped by the events—including the bullet graze to his head—he'd ridden into as soon as he hit town. He was hoping for a restful night's sleep, even though he was keenly aware of how few nights came and went without a visit by the nightmares that plagued him.

He took a long pull of the bourbon and tried not to think directly about that from which the nightmares had been born … in spite of what he focused on instead being so closely related. For within the Selkirk gang there was a man who had been involved in the butchering of The Lawyer's wife and children, the heinous act behind the nightmares and the shattering, life-changing deed that had re-set The Lawyer's course ever since.

The man's name was Jules Despare, a descendant of French pirates from the bayou country north of New Orleans. The Lawyer had gotten the lead on Despare from another participant in the slaughter, Lou Crenshaw, whom The Lawyer had caught up with down in south Texas. Crenshaw was the fourth of his family's killers he had tracked down and dispatched. Despare would be the fifth … and then there would only be two left.

As had been attempted previously, Crenshaw desperately tried to deal for his life at the last minute. In his case—although, like with the others, it ended up doing him no good—he coughed up the information on where The Lawyer could find Despare. Riding with the

Selkirk gang up in the northern part of the state. Pursuing that, The Lawyer had heard the news about the failed bank robbery and the incarceration of Ike Selkirk. His purpose in hastening to Emmett, then, had been the notion to somehow gain a one-on-one with Ike and try to get more detailed information on Despare's whereabouts. If it came down to it, The Lawyer had been fully prepared to break Ike out of jail himself in order to get him alone and do whatever it took to elicit what he wanted to know.

Only that opportunity got snatched away.

Yet one good thing came out of what had transpired instead. In the chaos surrounding the jailbreak, The Lawyer had laid eyes on Jules Despare. In the fleeting moment right before the grazing bullet knocked him down—that instant just as the rider he shot was spilling from his saddle—The Lawyer got a clear look at Despare. He was revealed to be *riding on the other side* of the man The Lawyer had just shot! The descriptions on him were too distinct for there to be any mistake— stringy blond hair, hawklike nose, and, most of all, the puckered red burn scar that included the lower half of where his left ear had been. The Lawyer saw these features as clearly as if the wild activity of the moment had suddenly frozen and he had all the time in the world to study the rider and make a positive identification. But, in truth, it only took a fraction of a second. Which, as it turned out, was all he had before the bullet skipped off the side of his head.

The mental image was in place, however, and it was branded deep. The irony wasn't lost on The Lawyer of how the man he was after had a scar on the left side of his face and now The Lawyer had one (although minor by comparison) of his own. A scar for a scar. If that's what it took, The Lawyer told himself, he would gladly trade a thousand scars to reach the final goal of catching up with the seven who had scarred him in ways no one could see yet reached all the way to his core and his soul.

The Lawyer's thoughts drifted to Doc Aarons's comments about the peculiarities of whipsawing luck. Having Ike Selkirk, the man he'd come here to see, broken out of jail within moments of his arrival had certainly seemed like a stroke of bad luck. But then, with the passage of only a few more moments, confirming that Despare not only was still part of the Selkirk gang but was now proven to be within reasonable proximity, had to be viewed as a good turn. The Lawyer felt confident he would have the piece of vermin in his grasp before much longer.

The fleeing outlaws would leave tracks.

The Lawyer had gotten quite good at tracking.

Extracting Despare from the others … there would be a way. He would find it. Even if it meant eliminating the rest of them to get at him.

The report brought back to town by Deputy Tell of finding one of the outlying lookouts with the back of his head bashed in and his throat slit from ear to ear not only reinforced how ruthlessly dangerous the Selkirk gang could be but it spoke with particular meaning to The Lawyer in that it suggested the personal touch of Despare, who was renowned for his use of bladed weapons, his favorite being a razor sharp Bowie knife. Which did nothing, of course, to dissuade The Lawyer from what he was bent on doing.

Lying still fully clothed atop the bed, The Lawyer took a final pull of the bourbon before drifting off to sleep. He hoped the nightmares would not come but fully expected that at some point they would.

CHAPTER FOUR

Ike Selkirk's wailing cut through the chill night air.

"Oww! Goddamn, that hurts! Maybe you'd like a pickaxe and a shovel so's you can go diggin' a little deeper!"

"Quit carryin' on so, you big baby," chided Lolena Tabor as she bent close over her task, squinting to see in the weak light of the lantern being held up by Ike's brother Owen. A cigarette was hanging out one corner of Lolena's mouth and as she spoke it bobbed up and down, sprinkling ash and the occasional spark onto the proceedings. She was a large woman with thick fingers and forearms, and shoulders as wide or wider than any of the men in the gang. Clad as she was in a pair of bib overalls and a flannel shirt, her form was thick but relatively shapeless except for the swell of massive breasts pushing against the bib straining to contain them. Her face, framed by an unruly spill of thick, iron gray hair, was wide and flat-featured in a way that hinted at some Indian blood running through her veins.

"Well that's my hide you're gougin' into, you know. Not the side of some damn mountain you're lookin' to pluck nuggets out of," continued to complain

Ike, himself a tall, barrel-chested, heavy-gutted specimen with a spikey black beard and a ledge of thick, connected brows above beady dark eyes.

Owen, a close replica to his older brother except for being stretched out longer and leaner, guffawed. "Oh, she's sure enough pluckin' out nuggets. And plenty of 'em. Hell, if they was the right kind we'd all be rich enough by now to never again have to worry about pullin' another bank job."

"Knock it off, you," growled Ike. "If you hadn't set a dynamite charge big enough to blow up half the goddamn town, I wouldn't have got peppered all up and down my whole backside like this!"

Ike was lying face down atop a horse blanket that had been spread on the ground. His shirt was removed and his britches were pulled part way down, exposing the ample twin moons of his pale, hairy butt. The bared length of him was deeply pock-marked by an irregular pattern of blood-rimmed dimples. From these, working with a pair of tweezers and the sharpened point of a jackknife, Lolena was methodically extracting jagged bits of stone that had once been part of his former jail cell's blasted back wall.

"We signaled you to lay low in that cell's far corner and pull your mattress over you for protection," Owen responded defensively. "I can't help it if that cheap Emmett jail supplied you with such a flimsy excuse for a mattress."

"Yeah, it was flimsy alright," Ike admitted grudgingly. "Damn near flimsy enough to end up servin' as a shroud to wrap me in if there'd been one more ounce of gunpowder in that dynamite."

"Well, there wasn't," snapped Lolena. "You're still alive and not behind bars no more. So be grateful we got you out and quit your bellyachin'."

It was full dark, except for the illumination thrown by the lantern and a nearby small campfire. The camp was well concealed, having been set up in a clump of hills nearly twenty miles to the north and west of Emmett—the same spot where the gang had holed up after the botched bank robbery and made their plans to go back and free Ike. Apart from those directly involved in picking the stone shrapnel out of Ike's back and butt, the remaining two gang members—Ben Mapes and Jules Despare—sat on either side of the nearby crackling fire. Mapes was sipping bitter coffee from a tin cup; Despare was absently honing the long, gleaming blade of his Bowie knife, a pursuit he never seemed to tire of. Occasionally the two men exchanged furtive grins at Ike's loudly voiced discomfort, but for the most part their expressions were neutral.

In response to Lolena's words about Ike still being alive, Mapes's long, wedge-shaped face pulled even longer with a look of pain and sadness. "Too bad the same can't be said for poor ol' Pedro," he muttered. "I rode a lot of years with that damn bean eater. Never could understand half of what he said, 'specially when he got excited and went to jabberin' in that damn Spanish lingo of his. But I took to likin' the little rascal all the same, and I sure hated leavin' him layin' back there in the dust."

"Yeah, I did too," Ike admitted. "And I'm grateful

he was part of comin' back to bust me out. That goes for all the rest of you, too, in case I ain't said it often enough … But, you know, that damn Pedro never could ride and duck at the same time worth shit. I tried to warn him a dozen times that if he didn't watch out he was gonna—Owww! Jesus Christ, woman, are you tryin' to poke that damn blade clear through my ass?"

"Aw, settle the hell down," Lolena said, grinning wickedly. "You've poked that bony skin blade of yours into my ass often enough, ain't you? And there was times you got to rammin' so hard I thought you was gonna shove it on through but you never heard me caterwallin' like a branded coyote, did you?"

"That's 'cause you was lovin' every minute," Ike said through clenched teeth.

"It's what you call an acquired taste," Lolena shot back. "Now I'm almost done here if you'll quit squirmin' around." She paused to issue a nasty laugh. "So shut up, hold still, and take it like a man."

When the last of the stone shards had finally been removed and some healing ointment smeared onto the wounds, Ike carefully hitched up his pants and walked gingerly over to be closer to the fire. Lolena followed behind, folding the blanket he'd been laying on into a thicker, softer pad and putting it down for him to sit on. Then she poured him a cup of coffee. This happened to be one of the stretches where Ike was the Selkirk brother she was sharing a bedroll with; so, as was Lolena's habit, despite her otherwise rough ways and words, she tended to be somewhat subservient to any man who was the "lover" in her life.

"Whew," said Ike, easing himself down on the blanket and shifting slightly to find a comfortable position. "This chewed up ass of mine is gonna make it mighty tough to cover very many miles in a saddle. The hard ride to make it this far damn near did me in."

"You figure on us ridin' away from here to somewhere else in particular, Ike?" asked Ben Mapes.

"Ain't decided, exactly," Ike responded. "But we can't stay holed up here for too long."

"You think that town will be sendin' a posse out after us, you mean?" said Jules Despare, the reddish scar tissue on the side of his face catching the light of the fire when he turned his head in a certain way, so that from time to time the puckered flesh seemed to glow with its own iridescence.

"Hell, I doubt that," spoke up Owen. "The way we blasted apart and shot up that place, I think the last thing anybody from there wants is to tangle with us again. Besides, we left their marshal and his deputy layin' dead in the middle of the street—who's left to even lead a posse?"

Despare shrugged. "Might be enough riled up citizens—exactly on account of the damage we *did* do—who'd pull together and make a try on their own, with or without any of 'em packin' a badge."

"I'd say that's a damn slim 'might'," argued Owen.

"If there was very many of 'em like that fancy-hatted bastard who shot Pedro," suggested Mapes, "it might not be such a slim prospect. Where the hell did he come from, anyway? I don't recall seeing him the first time, when they busted up our bank robbery attempt to begin with."

"Don't remind me about that first fiasco," Ike growled. "And who gives a damn about some jackass in a goofy hat who got off a lucky shot? I mean, apart from the fact that it turned out so bad for poor Pedro."

Despare made a face. "Maybe so. But I been thinkin' same as Ben. Something about that shooter and his hat keeps buggin' me."

"If you want to be bugged about something," said Ike, "then you might want to take into consideration how that Emmett marshal had more than one deputy. The second one wasn't there at the jail when ya'll blew it to hell. He'd gone home for supper and was due back to stand part of the overnight watch on me."

"So he might be the one to head up a posse to come after us. That what you're sayin'?" asked Owen.

"Mainly I'm just lettin' ya'll know he's there. It's something to keep in mind, that's all." Ike took a drink of his coffee, slurping loud. "I gotta add, though, there's a part of me wouldn't mind if he *did* head up a posse against us. One way or other, I wouldn't mind havin' another face-up with that sumbitch when I ain't held back by bars."

"Sounds like there was something about him that especially chapped your ass," remarked Lolena as she returned with a clean shirt to drape over Ike's shoulders.

"There sure was," Ike replied, the bitterness thick in his voice. "He was a goddamn *nigger*! Can you believe that? They stuck a badge on a stinkin' nigger and put him in a position to lord it over *white men* unfortunate

28

enough to land in that jail. Made my skin crawl and the bile rise up in my throat every second I was there."

CHAPTER FIVE

First thing the next morning, as promised, the maid who'd taken The Lawyer's soiled clothes for laundering came knocking on his hotel room door. When he answered, she held out the neatly folded evidence of her completed task. The Lawyer was impressed enough to tip her handsomely on top of the generous amount he'd already paid her ahead of time. And then, at her urging and insistence that she would take no further payment, he agreed for her to bring him a room service breakfast of fresh biscuits, a bowl of poached eggs, and a pot of coffee.

The Lawyer had been contemplating taking time for breakfast anyway, even though he was anxious to head out and pick up the trail of the jailbreakers as soon as possible. Especially since he now knew for certain that Jules Despare was riding in their midst. More than the matter of how long a meal would delay him, however, what had been giving him pause was the thought of how a visit to the hotel's dining room might possibly result in facing more eager back-patters looking to praise him for the way he'd so bravely dispatched one of the outlaws last night. So the offer of room service provided a welcome alternative.

When another tap came at the door only moments after the maid had departed, The Lawyer assumed the girl must have forgotten something. That assumption caused him to act in a very uncharacteristic way—he let down his guard. Without precaution, he simply pulled the door back open to see what she wanted.

Only it wasn't the maid standing there.

The Lawyer had no trouble recognizing the trim, muscular young black man who filled the doorway instead. It was Deputy Ernest Tell, whom he had met the previous night. On this occasion, The Lawyer immediately noticed two things different from their prior meeting: Tell was no longer wearing a deputy marshal's badge; and he was casually holding a Colt revolver at waist level, its muzzle angled upward so that it was aimed square at the center of The Lawyer's chest.

"Mornin', Mr. J.D. Miller," Tell greeted calmly. His gaze held steady. So did the gun muzzle.

The Lawyer gave as good as he got when it came to the stare-down that stretched over the next several beats. But, in the weapons department, he was sorely outmatched. His Remington was over on the bed, tucked under the just-delivered pile of fresh laundry, the way he'd slipped it out of sight in order not to alarm the maid.

"Or," Tell drawled on, "maybe I should just call you 'The Lawyer' … the way you're coming to be known by more and more folks, no matter what other name you hand out as an alias."

In point of fact, The Lawyer's true name *was* J.D.

Miller, not "J.D. Smith" like he'd signed the hotel register and told Doc Aarons. A lifetime ago, back before he'd begun the bloody trackdown of his family's butchers and gained notoriety as *The Lawyer*, J.D. Miller had actually been quite an accomplished attorney. But the retribution scourge he'd been on since that life was torn to shreds had entailed acts which, while clearly justified to his own mind, were not always in keeping with *proper* practices of the law. Subsequently, he himself had become an outlaw and a fugitive in the eyes of many and as a result had adopted some associated practices, using aliases included among them.

"I suppose," The Lawyer said now, "it would be useless for me to try and pretend I didn't know what you're talking about."

"Pretty much," Tell agreed. "I made a habit of closely studyin' all the wanted dodgers that came through the marshal's office. The ones on you I took a particular interest in. They gave a pretty good description, that's how I was able to identify you. Even at that, it didn't sink in right away—not with everything else that was goin' on last night. But, by the time I was ready to hit the sack, I had my mind made up who you were."

"Under different circumstances, I might find that a little flattering. But, as it is …"

"It just could be that circumstances ain't necessarily the way you're sizing 'em up," Tell suggested. He made a faint gesture with his gun barrel, then added, "How about you step on back into the room, real slow, and we can discuss things in more detail."

The Lawyer did as he was told, holding his hands out away from his body as he backed up, making sure to keep them in plain view. He was intrigued by Tell's words about things perhaps not being the way they seemed and also about that deputy's badge being conspicuously absent from the front of his shirt.

Tell followed him into the room in a long, gliding step. Heeled the door shut after he was in. "Go ahead, take a seat," he said, indicating with a tip of his head the room's single straight-backed chair over in one corner. "Rest your hands on your knees. Keep 'em in sight, like you have been. Just sit still and we'll get along fine."

The Lawyer sat, clamped his hands over his knees.

Tell's eyes made a quick scan of the room, lingering for a fraction of a second on the empty gun belt that lay in plain sight on the bed next to the saddlebags. Gaze snapping back to The Lawyer, he said, "Don't tell me you misplaced that fine Remington revolver that belongs in that equally fine tooled-leather holster."

Now it was The Lawyer's turn to motion with a tip his head. "Also there on the bed, under those freshly laundered clothes."

After spotting the gleam of gun metal peeking out from the pile and calculating the weapon to be sufficiently far enough out of The Lawyer's reach, Tell said, "Okay. That'll do."

"Do for what?" The Lawyer wanted to know, having trouble holding back a sudden surge of impatience fueled by anger for allowing himself to get cornered this way. "What's this all about? If you're going to arrest me, why not go ahead and get to it?"

With his free hand, Tell thumbed back the brim of his Stetson. A line of sweat beads stood out on his smooth, copper-brown forehead where the hat had been resting. The Lawyer wondered if this meant his captor wasn't quite as cool and collected as he outwardly appeared.

But, if that was true, there was nothing in his voice to indicate such when he said, "In case you ain't noticed—and I'd be surprised if you missed it—I'm no longer sportin' a deputy's badge. That's because I'm no longer a deputy, or lawman of any kind. So my reasons for bein' here got nothing to do with lookin' to make an arrest."

"The bounty on me, then?" The Lawyer said. "You turned in your badge to go independent and claim the price on my head?"

"Speakin' of heads—you ought to be careful about puttin' ideas like that in the noggin of a poor black man," Tell responded. "That thought hadn't occurred to me. But, if you give me time to think on it some, it might become a real temptin' notion."

"In that case, as they used to say in my former profession, strike that remark from the record."

"Consider it done."

The Lawyer regarded the man holding the gun on him. Surprisingly, he found himself starting to feel almost more curious than threatened. "So," he said, "that brings us right back around to where we were … What's your purpose here? What is it you want from me?"

"Answers. Plain and simple," Tell said. "And I got a hunch you ain't anxious to waste any more time about it than I am."

"You'd be right about that. What is it you want to know?"

"You can start by telling me what your interest in the Selkirk gang is. Like I said, I've done considerable reading about you and I'm confident on one thing: You wouldn't have messed in that business last night unless you came here with your sights already set on the Selkirk bunch, or at least one among 'em. You're locked cold and hard on the vengeance trail for those who slaughtered your family and it ain't your way to get side-tracked by good deed doin', not even throwin' a couple slugs at fleein' jailbreakers." Tell shook his head. "No, there's somebody in that outfit you've got an interest in or you wouldn't have allowed yourself to get involved, not even a whisker's worth."

"Apparently you're forgetting the fact I was crossing the street and they came riding straight at me. Ever consider I shot back out of self defense?"

Tell shook his head again. "Too pat. I ain't buyin' that. And the one you shot and killed—don't try to tell me he was the one you were out to get, either. I saw the way you acted afterward. When you looked down on him there was no hate in your eyes the way there would've been if he was one of your family's killers."

The Lawyer clenched his teeth. "You seem to have the questions *and* the answers, all on your own. Why bother me with any of it?"

"Then you admit I'm right so far?"

"I'll humor you. Say you are. That still doesn't tell me why you're here, what you want."

"All right. Let me give you some more answers. From my end … Ain't you wonderin' why I ain't a deputy no more?"

The Lawyer said nothing, just waited for him to continue.

"It's real simple. The fine folks of Emmett, you see, don't cotton much to a 'darky' upholdin' the law in their town—leastways not unless he's workin' under a white overseer. Hell, it ain't like I didn't have some notion of that all along. Especially in the beginning. I knew they only tolerated me because Marshal Ed said they should, because he saw something in me worth takin' a chance on. But after a year and a half doin' the job, sidin' the marshal and Deputy Dave and more than once layin' my neck on the line right alongside them, I was foolish enough to think I'd earned some measure of respect all my own."

Tell's eyes hardened, his gaze boring straight through The Lawyer by this point, seeing something known only to him. He went on, "But last night I found out quick enough how wrong I was, when I tried to muster up a posse to head out at first light this mornin' to go after the jailbreakers and killers. Oh, it wasn't that there weren't men on hand with enough courage to ride in a posse. There were those among 'em who'd done so plenty of times before … but *not* behind an 'uppity nigger.' And with the marshal and Deputy Dave layin' dead, that's all anybody saw me as."

"So they fired you as a deputy?"

"Fire me, be damned! I quit. Threw my badge in the dirt and told 'em all to go to hell."

The Lawyer gestured. "Yet here you are, pointing a gun at me."

Tell appeared to consider this, then gave a faint nod. "Fair enough," he said, holstering his Colt. "I reckon we can finish our talk with that out of the way."

"What's left to talk about?" The Lawyer asked. "You're going after the jailbreakers and killers on your own, right?"

"Damn betcha."

"For this town? After the way they've treated you?"

"Not hardly. Ain't doin' it for them. What I'm doin' is goin' after justice for the killin' of my friends. You ought to be able to understand that if anybody can."

The Lawyer's expression tightened.

"I ain't sayin' it's exactly the same," Tell quickly amended. "Didn't mean that Marshal Ed and Deputy Dave were dear to me in the way your family was to you. But they were still my friends. Especially the marshal. Like I said, he treated me like a man, gave me the chance to do something important, no matter the color of my skin. Deputy Dave, too. I could tell he wasn't crazy about partnerin' up with me at first, but he came around before long and we got on just fine … So they're the ones I'm doin' it for. Their killers deserve to be punished and I aim to be the one to see to it. And, since I ain't plannin' on givin' too much of a damn how I get it done, no longer packin' the weight of a badge might not be such a bad thing."

"I can understand that," The Lawyer allowed. "But

what I still don't understand is why you're telling it all to me."

"Let's keep on humorin' me. Let's pretend we both know you're goin' after that bunch, same as me. You want one in particular but I doubt you'd hesitate to take out any of the others who got in your way. I want 'em all and, especially since I don't know which is the one you're interested in, I don't figure to pick and choose when I start takin' 'em down. Wouldn't it make sense for us to go after 'em together?"

"I ride alone," The Lawyer said flatly.

Tell let out a sigh. Then one half of mouth twisted wryly. "Had a hunch you'd say that. I ain't one to beg, but I had to try. Leastways now you know I'll be out there on the trail, too. I hope we can keep from stumblin' over one another or gettin' in each other's way."

"Same here. I think you're probably a good man with good intentions, Tell, and I'll even wish you luck on what you're setting out to do." Here The Lawyer's expression turned as hard and cold as stone before he added, "Only make sure you understand this: I'll step around you and avoid stumbling over you if I can … But, if I have to, I won't hesitate to kill you if you get in the way of me doing what I have to do."

CHAPTER SIX

Tell was gone. The Lawyer had finished packing his saddlebags and was starting to regret he'd agreed to breakfast after all, when the maid returned with it. At her knock, he positioned himself off-center of the doorway with his right hand poised over the Remington now back in the holster of the gun belt buckled around his waist. He called out, asking who it was ... and then felt a little foolish when she answered.

He wolfed down the meal more quickly than he ordinarily would have, thoughts of the visit from the former deputy running through his mind as he did so. It had been a long time since The Lawyer allowed himself to develop a liking for anybody. His single-minded vengeance quest held no room for that kind of thing. And yet there *had* been a likability about the disillusioned yet fiercely determined Ernest Tell. Maybe it was just an appreciation of their mutual thirst for retribution, The Lawyer told himself. Whatever it was, it didn't really matter. He couldn't let it. As he'd made clear to the ex-lawman, he worked alone—and there was no room for changing that either.

Meal finished, The Lawyer quit his room and was

headed out through the hotel lobby when he ran into another interruption. It came in the form of three men who, it so happened, had just entered the establishment and were on their way to see him. All were middle-aged, somewhat soft-looking businessmen wearing suits, string ties, and earnest expressions. Each was fresh-faced and clean-shaven, to a man smelling faintly of talc and hair pomade.

The tallest of the trio and also the one exuding an air of being its leader looked vaguely familiar. He had a broad, fleshy face made to appear even broader by thick, snow white sideburns. The answer to why he seemed somewhat familiar came when he boomed out a greeting at the sight of The Lawyer. "Ah, Mr. Smith. How fortuitous, we came here looking for you. In case you don't remember—and it's certainly understandable if you don't, given all the chaos that was taking place—we met last night. My name is Alderdyce, I'm the mayor of our fair city. If you could spare my colleagues and me a moment, we'd like to have a few words with you."

Wondering (yet at the same time not really caring) what the hell this was about, The Lawyer said, "I'm actually in quite a hurry, gentlemen. I'm afraid I don't—"

"Surely you can spare a moment for us to state our business," Alderdyce said with the air of someone used to getting his way. "Then, should you find our proposal agreeable, we can discuss it further at a time more convenient to you."

"We can convene at that table over there," said one

of the other men, a gawky, rail-thin individual who pointed to a round-topped table over in one corner of the lobby, "where we will find a measure of privacy."

"Very well," The Lawyer allowed, figuring it was easier to relent slightly than to make an argument of it in the middle of the lobby. "But I'll warn you that I'm already involved in pressing business and I doubt I can be persuaded by any other proposal you might have."

Once seated at the table, The Lawyer found his time being wasted further by introductions to Alderdyce's colleagues. The first of these was a gawky man, Harris by name, a local realtor who doubled as the city attorney. Next was Samuelson, the portly, bourbon-nosed head of the local bank. When it came to the latter and the busy network of alcohol-induced veins exploding across the end of his snout, The Lawyer couldn't help thinking that here was someone into whose hands he surely would never trust his money. Had the recently attempted bank robbery been successful, The Lawyer cynically reflected further, he'd even go so far as to bet that a good deal of "mismanaged" funds might have conveniently been claimed as part of the take.

Sticking with thoughts of said robbery attempt, The Lawyer addressed Samuelson, saying, "From what I hear of recent events, you must be breathing quite a sigh of relief these days."

The banker smiled vaguely, even though it was clear the remark totally befuddled him.

With a weary air, as if explaining things to his liquor-addled colleague was becoming a tiresome habit, Alderdyce said, "He means because you're bank escaped being robbed by the Selkirk gang, Henry."

Samuelson's smile widened hazily. "Oh, that. Yes, yes, of course. I am quite relieved indeed."

Alderdyce shifted his attention back to The Lawyer. "It's appropriate you bring up the attempted robbery, Mr. Smith. You see, it—in a rather roundabout way—plays a part in our reason for coming here this morning."

The Lawyer said nothing, waited for the rest of it.

"Last night's jailbreak, as I know you are well aware by now," the mayor continued, "managed to free the gang leader who was apprehended during the failed attempt on the bank. That's one thing. That's bad enough. The real tragedy, of course, was the resulting deaths of our beloved town marshal, his chief deputy, and another of our brave citizens who was standing lookout duty outside of town."

The Lawyer nodded. "A tough thing, to be sure."

"Tough in more ways than one," spoke up Harris. "Not only for the grief and sadness of the fine lives lost but, in a broader sense, it leaves our town basically defenseless."

"From what I've seen and heard," The Lawyer replied, "you have more than a few townsmen—like the unfortunate lookout—who don't exactly run and hide at the first sign of trouble."

"True enough," agreed Alderdyce. "And that is something to take heart in and be proud of. But even the bravest, most well-intentioned men need a leader, an organizer, to get the best out of them. In matters of violence and the defense of our town and its laws,

Marshal Ed Maynard was that man. Sided, I must add, by a good right hand in young Dave Wilkes. Only now, unfortunately, both of them are suddenly gone."

"And that gang of ruthless savages is still out there," Banker Samuelson wailed.

The Lawyer frowned. "You think they might return—make another try for the bank, maybe look to take out some revenge on the whole town for giving them such a hard time?"

"Do *you* think that might be a possibility?" Alderdyce asked, fighting to control the anxiety in his voice.

The Lawyer considered for a moment. Then: "With a pack of scum like the Selkirks, anything is possible. On the one hand, they might see your town as being jinxed for them and never want anything more to do with it. The way it stands, they've still failed to make any money here and, even though they succeeded in busting one of their leaders out of your jail—*after* you managed to capture him in the first place, I'd add—it cost them the life of another gang member to do so."

"Thanks to you," Harris interjected.

The Lawyer shook his head. "Never mind that. The point is, it happened. But, on the other hand, all that bad luck just might add up to making them determined to return for payback. In the form of the bank money and more. And adding weight to that kind of thinking would also be the fact they can't help knowing they rode down and killed your marshal and chief deputy. Means they'll see your town as being in a weakened state, just as you yourselves are fretting over."

Samuels, the banker, looked ready to burst into tears.

Alderdyce looked grim. "You don't paint a very rosy picture."

"You asked," The Lawyer told him. "But, either way, you're not going to just take it, are you? I heard a Texas Ranger is due here any day, originally for the purpose of taking Ike Selkirk off your hands. And you've still got one deputy left, the young fella I met last night. Tell, isn't it?" The Lawyer already knew, of course, that Tell was out of the picture as far as representing the town, but he was curious to see how these city fathers would present their side of what had driven him out. He went on, "He should be able to mount a defense for your town, deputize the men he needs and so forth—at least temporarily, until the Ranger arrives."

Alderdyce and his colleagues exchanged uncomfortable glances.

"Thing is," The Lawyer went on, "I fail to under-stand why you came to me for all this speculation. I'm just a fella passing through who happened to hit town when all hell busted loose." He patted the saddlebags he had slung over one shoulder. "And, as you can see, that pressing business I already mentioned requires me to continue on."

"Yes, we can see that ... regrettably," the mayor said.

"Regrettably?" The Lawyer prodded.

"Oh, hell. Let's quit beating around the bush," said Harris, edging forward. "Mr. Smith, we came here to propose to you the notion of possibly serving as our town marshal. You demonstrated last night that you are a man of unquestionable bravery and that you are willing to take independent action, without hesitation, when called for. We feel those are exactly the qualities our town needs in a law officer."

"Plus," Alderdyce hastened to add, "those qualities have already impressed a large number of our constituents. We feel confident that such an appointment by us would be met with wide approval."

"What about Deputy Tell? What would he have to say about it?" The Lawyer wanted to know. "Seems to me he'd be a far more logical choice."

Again the exchange of uneasy glances, followed by an awkward silence.

Into which Samuels abruptly blurted, "But, if you met him last night, then surely you saw that he's a Negro. Did you not?"

The Lawyer clenched his teeth. "Wait a minute. Are you saying you'd be willing to bypass Tell, somebody already serving as a lawman for your town, in favor of me, basically a complete stranger—just because of the color of his skin?"

"Please understand," Harris responded, "those aren't necessarily our own feelings. But the late tragic war didn't end all that long ago and, in its aftermath, the simple facts are that the town of Emmett is made up of many Southern sympathizers, not to mention several men who fought under the Confederate flag. It is a foregone conclusion that any attempt to try and appoint Tell as marshal, even on a temporary basis, would be met with—"

"Then how the hell did he get a badge pinned on him to begin with?" The Lawyer demanded.

"Simply put, because Ed Maynard wanted it that way," Alderdyce answered. "Ed saw something in the boy. Not too many folks ever understood what. At any rate, with the marshal backing him, Tell became a deputy. But there was always added tension in any situation where he was involved, you could damn sure count on that."

"And," Harris added, "with Ed out of the picture, trust me, that tension would explode in no time. Even if Tell only stayed on as a deputy. Hell, what the Selkirk gang does or doesn't do would only—"

"What do you mean," The Lawyer interrupted, "*if* Tell stayed on as a deputy?"

Samuels made a sound not unlike a girlish giggle. "Oh, he's gone. Skedaddled. Say what you will about those darkies, there's still some of them who have the good sense to—"

"Shut up, Henry!" Alderdyce snapped, his face reddening with annoyance. Still scowling, he swung his attention back to The Lawyer. "It's true enough, though. Tell tried to form a posse last night, right after the bodies of Maynard and Wilkes had been cleared from the street. He was looking for men who'd commit to riding with him at first light to chase down the Selkirk bunch."

"Let me guess how many volunteers he got," The Lawyer said wryly, already knowing the answer.

Harris made a face. "That's right. If he'd ever had

any doubt before, he found out beyond question just how unpopular he was around here. So he threw his badge in the dust and told everybody in earshot that they could all go to hell and by his reckoning that would probably be too good for 'em."

The Lawyer smiled at this recounting. He also decided he had heard quite enough and wasted too much time listening to it. He stood up, saying, "Gentlemen—and rest assured I use that word very loosely—I not only am not interested in your proposal, I find it insulting and ridiculous. I must be on my way. And, for whatever it's worth, my sentiments upon departing you and your pathetic little town are pretty much the same as Deputy Tell's."

CHAPTER SEVEN

"Are you sure this idea of yours is a good one?" Owen Selkirk asked anxiously.

Sitting next to him before the crackling campfire, his older brother Ike took time for a sip of coffee from his tin cup before answering. When he did, his words came out in a vapor plume that trailed off in the crisp morning air. "If you mean am I absolute for certain it will work? No. You've been with me long enough to know that a body can never say for certain how these things will work out. Hell, we've seen enough of that lately, ain't we?"

"That's kinda my point."

"But it still don't mean *the idea* ain't a good one. It's bold and unexpected. You said last night that you figured the last thing anybody from that damn place would want was to tangle with us again. Well, I got a hunch they're thinkin' the same way about us—that the last thing *we* would want is to tangle with them again."

Owen twisted his mouth sourly. "For my part, they wouldn't be far off. I see that town as bein' bad luck for us and, I gotta say, I ain't real eager to take another run at it."

There was a hardened edge to Ike's voice when he said, "You makin' that a solid vote *against* the notion, little brother?"

Owen heaved a sigh, expelling his own elongated vapor plume. "No, I ain't sayin' that. No such. I'm just lettin' you know my feelings, that's all. You say we're gonna go with it, you know I'll back your play like always."

"I appreciate that, little brother, I surely do," Ike responded, his tone softening. "Shame on my sorry ass for not sayin' so often enough, but knowin' I can always count on you havin' my back takes a burden off my shoulders and is a great comfort to whatever our situation is."

On the other side of the fire, Lolena Tabor paused in the act of getting ready to light her cigarette with the flaming tip of a twig and said, "Jesus Christ you two, I hope the pair of you ain't getting ready to turn all sloppy and queer with brotherly love or something. You go that way on me, means I'd have to look to Mapes or ol' scar-faced Despare for my humpin'. Ain't neither one of 'em much to look at, but they say those Frenchies know some real interesting tricks when it comes to—"

"Knock it off with that shit," Ike cut her short. "I ain't in no mood. I'm still sore as hell from those two or three hunnert holes you gouged out all up and down my backside."

Lolena finished lighting her cigarette, then said, "If you'd let me smear some more of my salve on 'em, they'd start to heal a whole lot—"

"To hell with that salve of yours," Ike blurted, cutting her off again. "The way that shit burns, I might as well plop my ass down on the coals of this here campfire."

Lolena puffed smoke indifferently. "That might not be a bad idea, neither. You've heard about cauterizin', right?"

"Speakin' of Mapes and Despare," Owen cut in before the barbs flying back and forth got any sharper, "oughtn't they be getting back before much longer?"

Ike took time to scratch vigorously under his chin, nails rustling loudly through the coarse whiskers there. Then he said, "I sent 'em out before first light, told 'em to make a wide sweep across our back trail. Take a good hard look for any sign of a posse who might be sniffin' around out there but be sure they didn't get their own asses spotted while they was at it. So it would've took a while. But, yeah, they oughta be showin' up pretty soon."

"You sent 'em out early right enough, 'fore they had a chance for any breakfast," Lolena noted. "Reckon I should have a fresh pot of coffee ready and fry up some bacon for when they get back. Speakin' of which, we're runnin' mighty thin on rations. When we started out on this little do-se-do, nobody figured on it draggin' out for so long."

"No shit," Ike grunted.

"Don't get huffy with me about it," Lolena snapped back. "I'm just sayin', that's all. Whatever we're gonna do, we're gonna need some food for our bellies. And, in case you ain't noticed, we've also burnt up a hell of a lot of our ammunition. Hell, we got more firepower left in dynamite than we do in cartridges. Happens we somehow get ourselves cornered and have to try and shoot our way out again, we'll be hurtin'."

"She's pointin' out some facts we have to take into consideration, big brother," said Owen.

"Yeah, yeah. I know." Ike threw down the last of his coffee before adding, "Sorry I snapped at you, Lolena darlin'. A body hates to hear bad news, that's all—especially when it comes in piles."

"Ain't like it's nothing we can't fix," Lolena replied. "We just need to recognize it and take some necessary steps before it puts us in a pinch."

"Far as food," said Owen, "there's bound to be some good-sized ranches around here where they're sure to have plenty of basics like coffee and bacon we could relieve 'em of. And, if they got a decent-sized crew of wranglers, likely most of them fire .44-40 cartridges for both their handguns and rifles. Same as us. We could hit a place like that in the middle of the day, while most everybody was out workin' cattle, and heal up our needs easy as pie."

Ike cocked an eyebrow. "You know, that ain't a half bad idea. Thing is, though, if we go that way then we'll have to be prepared to hit the bank right quick afterwards—before word spreads about us still bein' in the area and we find those damn Emmett townies primed for us all over again."

"That's fine by me," allowed Owen. "If you're bound and determined to take another stab at it—and I've already told you I'll follow your lead—then I'm all for gettin' it over as quick as possible."

Ike twisted his mouth wryly. "But you still think the place holds a jinx for us, don't you?"

"No need to keep chewin' that cud." Owen set his jaw firmly. "I told you I'd go along with you, what more do you want me to say?"

"Well, what I got to say," spoke up Lolena as she forked thick slabs of bacon into a heavy iron skillet, "is that you two better get your heads screwed on straight and make sure they're pointed in the same direction if you want to give us our best chance for success."

"Don't worry about us, woman," Ike snapped. "Comes time to do our work, you can bet the Selkirk boys will be pullin' in the harness together."

Not long after, Mapes and Despare hove into sight, approaching the camp at a steady gallop. Their appearance was timed almost perfectly to Lolena's removal of the first of the now crisply fried bacon strips.

Ike waited until the returning men had dismounted, ground-reined their horses, and reached gratefully for cups of steaming coffee that Lolena held out to them. Then, somewhat impatiently, he said, "Well? What did you come across out there?"

Mapes shook his head. "No sign of a posse, if that's what you mean. Not a hint."

"How close to the town did you venture?"

"Within six-eight miles." Mapes turned his head and said to Despare, "Wouldn't you say that's about right?"

The Frenchman nodded as he took the pieces of bacon on a slab of hardtack that Lolena was handing him. "About that, yeah. Maybe a tad closer, but not much."

A smug look spread across Ike's face. "Just like we figured. What a bunch of chickenshits. Real brave when they had us boxed up in the middle of the street, out-gunned a dozen to one. But havin' the guts to come out and face us in the open, that's quite a different thing for the gutless bastards."

"I said we didn't see no sign of a posse," Mapes reminded him as he took a chomp of his own bacon and hardtack. Then, working to get more words out around the oversized bite, he added, "But we did see a strange sight that involved a handful of riders."

"What the hell's he talking about?" Ike demanded, pinning Despare with a scowl. "I can hardly understand the slob with his mouth crammed full like that. Did he say you ran into some riders out there?"

"We didn't run into 'em. Which is to say they didn't see us," Despare answered. "But yeah, back toward town we spotted four riders in a stand of brush and boulders on the slope of a spiney ridge. Kinda looked like they'd just got there and were waiting for some-thing."

"Waiting for what? There ain't no stage or nothing goes in and out of that town to the north, is there?"

"Not that I know of. Even if there was, they wasn't by any kind of road. They was off-trail, sorta on the path we took tearin' out last night."

"You mean they was trackin' us?"

"If they were, they had a funny way of doing it. Just sitting there waiting like that, I mean."

With his mouthful of food mostly swallowed now, Mapes said, "I figure it was more like they just *happened* to be nearby where we passed. Whatever they're up to, curious as it seemed, I don't think it's got anything to do with us. Just to be sure, though, when me and Despare cut away from there, we swung plenty wide and made sure we took to as much rocky ground as we could so's to make certain we didn't leave no fresh tracks for nobody."

"Okay. That part was good thinking," Ike allowed. Then he asked, "While you was ridin' around out there, did you happen to spot any sign of a close by ranch?"

Mapes frowned. "Yeah, matter of fact we rode in sight of a couple of 'em. One small, one that looked pretty good sized. Mind if I ask why you want to know that?"

"Because," Ike said, "we're gonna be payin' a visit to one of 'em. The bigger one, most likely."

"What for? We goin' in the rustling business now?"

"We're gonna rustle some things from a ranch, yeah," said Owen. "But no stinkin' cattle. They're too much work."

"We're goin' after supplies," Lolena chimed in. "Supplies for our bellies and supplies for something to make sure our shootin' irons can keep shootin'."

Despare's eyebrows lifted. "And, after that, do I small a new job being cooked up?"

"Already cooked, Frenchy," Ike told him. "We're goin' back to that townful of chickenshits who are hidin' behind closed doors and under their beds and hopin' like hell they never see the likes of us again. But they're gonna see us all the same, and this time Emmett's stubborn damn bank is gonna cough up a nice, fat wad of money for us."

"By God, I like the sound of that!" said Mapes with so much enthusiasm he sprayed hardtack crumbs out his mouth. "We've rode in and out of that shithole of a town twice now and always made it out *minus* something—one of our own each time, and last night one of 'em permanent. This time we'll be the ones who do the subtracting and I say we pick the bastards clean!"

CHAPTER EIGHT

"How can we be sure he'll come this way?" groaned a badly hung over Danny Purl, wincing painfully as he glanced back toward town and inadvertently caught a glint of bright, early sunlight that stabbed like a knife into his already aching brain. "Hell, for that matter, how can we be sure he'll be riding out at all this morning?"

Danny was leaning on a low, weather-rounded boulder, steadying himself against the queasiness in his gut that ached nearly as bad as his head and threatened to hurl—not for the first time—whatever contents were left inside him. He was a thin, rawboned youth, several months short of twenty, dressed in wrangler's clothes. At the moment, his normally ruddy complexion was more of a fish belly white tinged with green.

"You heard him last night," answered Curly Krebs from a few feet off to Danny's right on the southern slope of a rocky, brushy ridge. Curly was a half dozen years older, stocky of build, mean-eyed and lantern-jawed with a wide mouth that seemed perpetually curled into a sneer. He was standing in a relaxed manner, tipped back against a tall, slanted boulder with a long-necked, half-empty bottle of whiskey dangling from the fingers of one hand.

"After he failed to drum up any takers for ridin' out in a posse with him at first light," Curly continued, "you heard how he told everybody to go to hell then threw his badge to the ground and announced he'd be goin' after the Selkirk gang all on his own. You think he can back out on a follow-through after blowin' in front of everybody that way? No, he might only *pretend* to ride out on a trackdown of the Selkirks, but he'll go along with the act at least that far. And since too many folks in town saw the gang tearin' off in this direction, he ain't got no choice but to head this way."

"Well, whatever he's gonna do," moaned Danny, "I wish he'd hurry up and show. All I want is to finish our business with him so I can decide if I'm fit to crawl off somewhere and try to heal, or just curl up and die."

Earl Brewster emerged from some nearby bushes, refastening the last button on the front of his trousers. He was a tall, angular man with a pronounced Adam's apple and the rolling, bow-legged gait of someone who had spent decades on horseback. As he approached the two younger men, he hacked up a gob of phlegm and spat it away over his shoulder. "There," he exclaimed in a raspy voice, "now that I've made room by empty-ing my bladder and got the cobwebs cleared out of my throat, I'm ready for another snort of that who-hit-John you got there, Curly."

Hearing this, Danny groaned louder than ever. "Good God Almighty, after we damn near drained the saloons dry and then kept on drinkin' away the rest of the night, I don't know how you fellas can stand another swallow of that rotgut."

"See, that's your trouble, Danny Boy," said Brewster as he reached out and deftly caught the bottle Curly tossed his way. "You cut back on your drinkin' and started to sober up. That's a sure fire road to the miseries of bein' hung over. You gotta stick with pettin' the hair of the dog, as they say. Stay a little tippled all the time, you plumb keep the miseries away."

From higher up on the slanted boulder, where he was peering out through a lookout notch near the peak, Bob Felker, the final member of the group called down. "If that's the last bottle of hooch you're tossin' around down there, you'd damn well better save some for me. And with the kid pukin' every five minutes and Brewster pissin' and hackin' up pieces of his lung, if I climb down and step in a pile of slop that belongs in somebody's insides, I'm apt to use that bottle on the outside of a couple damn skulls."

Felker was a burly number with a bent nose and thick scar tissue around his eyes that spoke of a brawling background. And the fire smoldering in those dark, dangerous, scar-encircled eyes suggested he likely hadn't come up short in very many of those conflicts. This current undertaking may have been started at the urging of Curly, but everybody involved had a clear understanding that Felker didn't make a habit of being a follower, not to anybody.

"Skull thumpin' ain't gonna be the half of it," Curly snarled viciously, "when that goddamn Tell finally pokes his head into sight. Recent times, him and his uppity manner been tolerated as long as he had a badge and Marshal Ed to hide behind, gave serious grief to each and every one of us. Well those days are done, by God, and now it's time for some payback."

"Amen to that, brother," rasped Brewster. "Black bastard laid a gun barrel across the side of my head one night when I was raisin' hell in the Lucky Dog. Which sure as blazes wasn't lucky for me that night. Anyway, it cracked my jaw and broke off a wisdom tooth that later on took ol' Doc Himple a full hour—an hour of pure hell for me, I'll tell you—to get the root dug out the rest of the way. I maybe had a rap on the noggin comin' … But not from no stinkin' darky. I ain't forgot about it, not by a long shot. I always figured the day'd come for my chance to get even."

"Well it looks like today's your lucky day," spoke Felker from high up on the slanted boulder. "If I ain't mistaken, I see former deputy Tell ridin' our way now."

* * *

The sound of distant gunfire had lasted for ten or fifteen minutes before abruptly ending. Under different circumstances, once he'd made sure the shooting wasn't aimed at him, The Lawyer would have taken measures to circle wide and avoid getting caught up in somebody else's trouble. But a chance the Selkirk gang, including Jules Despare, could unexpectedly be still in the vicinity and the shooting might somehow be related to them, this time made it a matter he couldn't risk avoiding.

The Lawyer reckoned he had reached a point about eight or nine miles north of Emmett. In addition to seeing which way the gang headed as they barreled out of town, he'd had no trouble following the way they continued once in the clear. So far, north and slightly west was their unwavering course. It was plain enough to present hardly any challenge to the tracking expertise The Lawyer had developed since setting out after the killers of his family. There were, however, some rather curious added features that a less skilled set of eyes may have missed.

For starters, other horses—four of them—had more recently passed the same way. And then, even more recently, a single horse had ridden over the same ground. The latter was probably Ernest Tell, The Lawyer told himself. No surprise there. But what of the four riders in between? Following Tell's failure to raise a posse, neither his own account nor that of Alderdyce and his colleagues had mentioned anything about an alternative force gathering to take up the chase. That didn't mean such a thing couldn't still have happened, though. If so, it raised the possibility that those horsemen—or Tell, for that matter—might be part of the shooting The Lawyer heard. All of which only gave more impetus to investigating what was behind it.

The crackle of gunfire had come from off to the northeast, somewhere along the spine of a boulder- and brush-strewn ridge that twisted away in that general direction. From where he sat his saddle, The Lawyer could see no sign of gunsmoke haze and—although the terrain could be somewhat sound-distorting—the shots hadn't seemed immediately close. Based on this, he reined Redemption sharply and gigged the Morgan mare straight for the ridge at a hard clip. Reaching the base of the nearest slope, he dismounted, gave Redemption a firm stay command, and then proceeded on foot with Remington drawn and ready.

Ascending to the crest of the ridge, The Lawyer began following it toward where he judged the shooting had originated. He moved quickly and quietly, sticking as much as possible to the cover of the bushes and various-sized boulders, as well as the smattering of scraggly trees. He paused periodically to listen, hearing little but the low moan of a breeze that skimmed up from the surrounding smoother, grassy hills.

And then, considerably closer than he'd expected, The Lawyer came in sight of what appeared to be those responsible for the shooting he'd heard. On the back side of the ridge, down on the flat a short distance out from a sharp drop-off caused by an ages old wash-out, four men were gathered around a twisted cottonwood tree that stood incongruously tall and alone, jutting up from the rocky ground.

One of the men was holding himself awkwardly, unsteadily, as if injured. When he turned a certain way, The Lawyer saw a large blood stain on the front of his shirt; little doubt the result of a bullet wound. Some horses were ground reined a short distance away and, across the back of one of them, the limp, still form of a fifth man lay face down. Back over by the cottonwood, two of the remaining men stood beside another horse positioned under the twisted branches. They were struggling to hoist a third man onto the back of the horse. As The Lawyer watched, they succeeded in getting him up into the saddle while the wounded man unsteadily held a gun on him. The now-mounted man had his hands tied behind his back and he, too, was streaked with blood and dust. Not from a bullet wound, though—at least that was the judgment of The Lawyer, now that he was able to get a good look—but rather from having endured a brutal beating.

The man in question was Ernest Tell. What was more, The Lawyer realized with a start, in addition to being beaten and wrist-tied he had one end of a long rope knotted around his neck. Its opposite end was flung up and over the cottonwood's thickest horizontal branch and left dangling down alongside the trunk. What was about to happen next was agonizingly clear.

Cursing under his breath, The Lawyer began making his way down the edge of the wash-out. Luckily he wasn't the only one cursing—Tell's captors were unleashing a foul-mouthed tirade against him that grew steadily louder in The Lawyer's ears as he drew closer. That was the good news, the fact the men were laying on their verbal abuse so thick it effectively drowned out the sounds of his descent, allowing him to approach almost recklessly and still go unheard and unnoticed. The bad news was that, even as they ranted and raved, one of the would-be hangmen was tying the free end of the rope around the trunk of the cottonwood. Once it was secured, that would leave only a hand-slap of time—the instant it would take to smack the horse on the rump and send it bolting out from under its restrained rider—before Tell was swinging by his neck.

From the angle of his descent, even if he'd stopped

and taken his most careful aim, The Lawyer had no clear shot at the man doing the tying-off. As he stumbled out onto the flat, he was still over twenty yards away from where Tell sagged in the saddle, all the slack pulled out of the noose around his neck. And, at that same moment, the man who'd removed said slack and tied off the free end of the rope straightened triumphantly from the task. Any attempt by The Lawyer to shoot or shout for a halt at that point would only have provided a possible assist by alarming the horse and causing it to lunge away.

But then, only a fraction of a second later, that became a moot point.

The wounded man who'd been keeping Tell rather unsteadily covered abruptly aimed his gun skyward and fired off two rapid rounds. The horse bolted. The two men who'd hoisted Tell up into the saddle encouraged the animal on its way with high-pitched screeches of "Yeeehaw!"

That left The Lawyer, still unnoticed by the team of hangmen, only one chance to try and save the man at the end of the rope. He dropped a knee to the dirt, raised his Remington revolver, steadied it, took half a breath and held it, set his aim on the swaying rope and began firing. The first shot missed completely. The second nipped away some fibers. The third hit dead center, severing the rest of the interwoven strands.

Tell toppled heavily to the ground.

The two men closest to where he fell wheeled about, eyes wide with surprise but then quickly narrowing above angrily twisted mouths that spat new curses.

The third man, the wounded one, also turned to face The Lawyer but did so slowly and with added unsteadiness, as if the exertion of firing off the two shots had weakened him all the more. Even though he already had his gun drawn, he registered as the lowest priority to be reckoned with. The Lawyer had three bullets left to deal with three proven killers and he had to make sure he put them where they'd count the most.

Remaining on one knee as the hands of the two angry-eyed men stabbed downward, reaching for their own holstered pistols, The Lawyer snapped off a pair of rounds almost simultaneously. The slug from each scored a head impact. The first victim, a lanky, bow-legged number, fell straight back, his shoulders hitting the ground flat as a geyser of blood, skull splinters, and brain matter arced upward. The second man, stocky and sneering, spun away before falling, also gushing blood and gore from the outward-erupting exit hole in the back of his head.

The Lawyer swung his Remington and brought it to bear on the wounded man, the only one left. The Lawyer saw that he was barely more than a boy and that he was already in a bad way. His face was deathly pale, beaded with pain-fueled sweat. The stain on the front of him was fresh and wet and growing larger, made so by weakly pumping blood. The arm he was trying to raise in order to aim his gun trembled with the effort.

"Don't do it, boy. Let it drop," The Lawyer told him. "You may still have a chance."

The youth made no reply, but his arm kept lifting, ever so slowly. The distance between them was too great to try and rush him yet too close to risk that his aim, trembling though it might be, would prove harmless.

The Lawyer held off as long as he could before spending the final bullet in his Remington.

CHAPTER NINE

"They were waitin' for me back near the trail left by the Selkirk gang," Ernest Tell explained. "I'd spotted that there were other tracks mixed in with the Selkirks', but hadn't figured out what to make of 'em. When I got close to where they were layin' up, this bunch rode out into plain sight and waved me down, all friendly-actin'. Said they wanted to ride with me after the jailbreakers and killers, but hadn't spoke up back in town for fear of gettin' a hard time from the other fellas. They fooled me good, I should have seen through 'em right away, but I guess I was either too stupid or too desperate."

The Lawyer had assisted the beaten man once more into a saddle, this time the one cinched to his own Appaloosa gelding, before walking horse and rider back to where he'd left Redemption. From his possibles pack The Lawyer had taken bandages and medicinal salve and then, after easing the man off the Appaloosa and double-checking to make sure he had no broken bones or more serious injuries, he began cleaning and dressing the worst of the cuts and bruises.

"After I let 'em get in close around me," Tell went on, "they jumped me. Dragged me down, stripped away my gun, and commenced beatin' the holy hell outta me."

"You know any of them?" The Lawyer asked.

"Knew 'em all ... Well, except for that skinny kid. Reckon he was a new rider for one of the cattle ranches in the area. Guess I might've seen him around town a time or two but he never caused any trouble before ... I heard a couple of the others call him Danny."

"And the others were all wranglers?"

"Uh-huh. Typical 'punchers who'd show up in town after bein' paid, sometimes get too drunk and then too rowdy. To the point where they'd have to be hauled down and thrown in the clink until they sobered up and were ready to act sensible again. I'd had run-ins with all three of the others in recent months. Called for me to smack 'em down and haul 'em off."

"That was their beef with you? That you had to tame them down when they got out of hand?"

"What more did they need?" Tell said bitterly. "Black man hidin' behind a badge, havin' the gall to put *them* behind bars. And now that I no longer had a badge to hide behind."

"For *that* they were going to hang you?"

Tell shook his head. "I don't know that they actually set out to take it that far, but the one called Felker was awful good with his fists. He started layin' in some mighty hard punches, threatenin' to do real damage. I guess I panicked. When he made the mistake of leanin' in too close, I grabbed the gun out of his holster and shot my way clear. I wasn't aimin' to kill, just to back 'em off me. But Felker moved in a way I didn't expect and one of my slugs drilled him straight in the heart. He was dead before he hit the ground.

"It turned into a kind of runnin' battle for a little while after that. I made for the ridge to try and gain cover. But Felker's gun was a .45, all I had in my shell belt was .44 cartridges. I managed to wound the skinny kid before I ran out of bullets. Then they swarmed me again. Their blood was really up by then and that's when the one called Curly said I was ripe for hangin' from the nearest suitable tree. The other two didn't disagree."

The Lawyer rocked back on his heels and examined his patchwork. "Well, they should have. For their own sake," he said. "Nothing to be done for them now. But I figure you're going to make it okay. You'll be sore as blazes for a time, but I don't think there's any serious damage."

"Thanks to you. And I mean for a lot more than just the bandaging."

"The way it turned out, that's all," The Lawyer said, downplaying his role. "I could hardly let them hang you."

"Why not?" Tell wanted to know. "They was just gettin' even for what I did to their friend."

"You know better than that. What you did was self-defense—against something that was wrong and unwarranted in the first place. What they tried to do to you came from pure, lowdown hatred. Hatred for the color of your skin, the thing that was pushing them from the start."

"Yeah, I know about that well enough. Been

runnin' into it, one way or other, about as long as I can remember." Tell absently touched fingertips to his throat, gently probing the bandage now covering the raw, salved-over rope burns there. "But I still can't keep from wonderin' about something."

The Lawyer produced a flask of whiskey from his possibles pack and held it out, saying, "For medicinal purposes. My final bit of treatment."

"Much obliged," said Tell, taking the flask and wasting no time tipping it high and taking a long pull.

"So what is it you can't keep from wondering about?"

Lowering the flask, Tell answered, "When you find yourself with a rope around your neck and it looks like you're only a second or two away from dyin', it's surprisin' the kinds of things that run through your head. What it came down to, for me, was that I kept questionin' this thing I've set out to do … Huntin' down the killers of Marshal Ed and Dave. Callin' it justice when what I'm really after is revenge. That's why I said back in your hotel room that it was a relief not to be packin' a badge anymore. If justice is what I'm after—the *Law's* kind of justice—then I shouldn't be feelin' that way, should I?"

The Lawyer gave him a look. "You really think I'm the best person to ask that question? But don't think I haven't asked myself some version of the same thing plenty of times in recent years. As an attorney, remember, I used to stand hard and fast for justice according to the law. By definition, and in the eyes of most people, justice is the administration of just and deserved punishment in accordance with some kind of legal ruling."

Holding his hand out for the flask and taking his own pull from it, The Lawyer then continued. "Vengeance is the infliction of harm or injury in return for injury. Retribution is to retaliate according to deserts ... I could go on, but I think you see the pattern. Take away the part about a legal ruling, they're all cut from similar cloth. And when you consider how complex laws are getting to be and therefore how they can be misinterpreted, manipulated, and too often downright corrupted, well, it's understandable how some men might see the straightest, surest path to satisfactory justice can only be one they map out for themselves."

By the time he'd finished, The Lawyer's eyes had grown harder and narrower, his voice somewhat remote. Listening to him, watching him, Tell felt a curious certainty that what he'd just heard amounted to the closing argument with which The Lawyer had decided on the course he would take for responding to the slaughter of his wife and children. And, for his part, it also served to reaffirm the former deputy's own determination on how he meant to deal with those who'd killed his friends.

Clearing his throat, he said, "So then. I guess the thing now is to try and make up for some of the time that got lost due to my spot of trouble, and get on with our other business."

The Lawyer cut him a sidelong glance. "I have no problem with the 'getting on' part. But it doesn't apply to you, you stubborn fool. Not right away. When I said I figured you were going to make it okay, I meant make it back to Emmett so you could check in with Doc Aarons. No way of knowing for sure that beating didn't tear you up inside. You need to find out about that from a professional."

"Uh-uh. That ain't gonna happen." Tell set his jaw determinedly. "You fixed me up good enough. I'm continuin' on after that Selkirk bunch and not wastin' no more time about it. Besides, goin' back to Emmett would only give the next handful of rowdies an excuse to try and settle a score with me."

"If you're worried about tangling with a rowdy," said The Lawyer through clenched teeth, "then you might want to think about looking closer than—"

He stopped short, scowling at the expression that had suddenly gripped Tell's face and the way he was peering intently off to the north. Turning, The Lawyer followed the ex-deputy's line of vision in order to see for himself what was going on.

CHAPTER TEN

"It's them, I tell you. I spotted 'em and recognized 'em the first time they showed up, didn't I? Why would I not know what I saw this time?"

The man doing the talking was named Wil Thornberry, a reclusive old prospector who roamed the hills and open country to the north of Emmett. As he had just reminded everybody, he was the one who'd seen and reported the presence of the Selkirk gang when they first arrived in the area—in time for Marshal Maynard to prepare a welcoming committee for them when they tried to hit the Emmett bank. And now here Thornberry was again, having suddenly appeared out of nowhere to interrupt the argument between The Lawyer and Tell, in a lather to once more report a sighting of the Selkirk bunch.

"Okay, okay. Try to take it easy," Tell urged him. "You say you saw the Selkirks again, nobody's claimin' otherwise. And it was up at the Box-U spread where you spotted 'em?"

"Uh-huh. Not more'n an hour ago." The old man's weathered, whiskered face was a mask of anguish. "I saw 'em and, oh Lord, I wish I never had. Those men and that thing what passes for a woman who rides with 'em—they're demons straight outta Hell and that's where they need to be sent back to. I thought at least part of 'em would be on their way by now, from the last time I warned about 'em bein' hereabouts."

"Their day is coming, old timer. Rest assured on that," The Lawyer promised him.

Thornberry's rheumy eyes looked like they wanted some hope to cling to, but remained unconvinced. "How can you claim that? Ya'll just got done tellin' me the marshal and his chief deputy are dead, gunned down and trampled by these devils. Who's gonna face 'em now?"

"We are," said Tell.

Thornberry looked no less forlorn. "Just the two of you?"

For a moment it was as if The Lawyer and Tell momentarily forgot about the old prospector. They locked eyes and held like that for several beats. Until, in a low, steady tone, The Lawyer finally said, "That's right ... the two of us."

* * *

The way Thornberry told it, he had gone to the Box-U Ranch shortly after daybreak. It was widely known that, apart from swinging a mean pickaxe and shovel, the old prospector had a knack for brewing up some of the finest moonshine to be found anywhere in the territory. One of his regular stops for selling off part of his product was with Ollie Fennergan, the bunkhouse cook for the Box-U, and that's what had brought Thornberry around this morning. As was his habit, he waited until the ranch crew had finished breakfast and ridden out to for the day's work (this morning there was branding to be done). After the hungry wranglers were out of the way, Thornberry could usually mooch a late breakfast for himself.

This time, however, Thornberry found Ollie in no condition to be preparing him anything—not this morning, not ever again. The cook was sprawled on the floor of his kitchen in a huge puddle of his own blood, throat slashed wide open like a second gaping mouth.

"Despare again," The Lawyer had muttered in a low, harsh tone upon hearing this part. Naturally, Thornberry didn't have to see much more to be alerted and alarmed that there was something badly wrong at the Box-U Ranch. After discovering Ollie, he crept cautiously out through the bunkhouse to try and get a better idea what had led to such a thing.

The front door of the bunkhouse was hanging ajar. Careful not to reveal himself to anyone on the outside, Thornberry had made his way to the opening and peered through it to see what else he could make out. Over by the tool shed, beside a wagon they apparently had been working on, he spotted the bodies of two ranch hands who looked to have been shot. The old prospector was sweeping his gaze slowly over the rest of the grounds when he heard the screaming—faintly at first—coming from the main house.

And then, as the screams grew louder, he saw the eighteen-year-old daughter of ranch owner Gustav Urlanger and his wife Harriet burst out the side door and go running blindly across the scrubby grass. The girl was stripped nearly naked, save for a few bits of torn flimsiness fluttering around her thighs and ankles. Her face and arms reddened with fresh bruises.

As Thornberry watched, stunned by what he was witnessing and too afraid to try and do anything about it, two men came running in pursuit of the girl. He recognized both of them from his previous encounter with the Selkirk gang. One was none other than Owen Selkirk, the youngest brother. Thornberry had never heard a name for the other, but the bright pink burn scar on the side of his face made him unmistakable. At present, he was also shirtless with one of his suspender straps fallen down and dangling uselessly as he ran.

The girl didn't get far before the pair caught up with her and dragged her roughly to the ground. Owen dropped to his knees near the girl's head, laughing wildly as he grabbed her flailing arms and pinned them down. While he was doing this, the shirtless man dropped partly onto the girl, wedging himself between her legs, pawing and cursing her for what her attempted escape had clearly interrupted. And then he mounted her and commenced his rutting right there on the dusty grass, goaded in the act by Owen who continued to help hold her. The girl's screams turned to helpless sobs.

Thornberry turned away, unable to watch any more. As he did so, he was aware of more screams, those of a new voice—that of Harriet Urlanger, the mother, he supposed—coming from inside the house. The old prospector stumbled out the back door of the bunkhouse kitchen and climbed into the saddle of his horse. He left his pack burro behind and spurred as hard as he could for the town of Emmett, meaning to report the horror taking place at the Box-U and hope to God someone could make it back in time to do some good for those poor women, keep them from ending up as dead as poor Ollie and the other men he had seen.

Upon first running into The Lawyer and Tell and giving his story to them, Thornberry had initially held little hope that only the two of them would be enough. Once they'd ridden off in the direction of the Box-U, however, after encouraging him to go on to Emmett and see what additional help he could raise there, he kept remembering the stony looks on the faces of the two men as they wheeled their horses and bolted away ... Continuing to contemplate this as he galloped on toward town, Thornberry got to thinking that maybe his initial assessment had given too short a shrift to the pair. One thing he decided for by-God certain: *He* wouldn't want to be anybody those two were riding to confront.

CHAPTER ELEVEN

"Well, we got our supplies restocked and then some," Lolena Talbot was saying. Cigarette smoke curled out the corners of her mouth and wrapped around her words. "We can leave here any time you say the word."

She was sitting with Ike Selkirk at the dining room table of the well-appointed Urlanger home at the Box-U ranch. Fine furnishings surrounded them. Piled in the center of the table were three canvas bags bulging with the food and cartridges stuffed into them. Seated on the other side of the bags, sipping from a decanter of fine brandy, Ike wore a distracted expression and seemed lost in thought.

"You figure on headin' out and takin' another stab at that bank yet today, didn't you?" Lolena prompted, raising her voice to gain his attention.

Ike swung his eyes to her and blinked a couple times, getting re-focused. "We ain't gonna just *take* a stab at that stinkin' goddamn joint," he snarled, "we're gonna gut it wide open and claw its insides till it's bled dry."

"Fine by me. But I repeat: When you figurin' on doin' that?"

"We'll do about like ya'll did when you busted me out of their damn jail … We'll hit 'em late in the afternoon, when everybody's gettin' slow and lazy and thinkin' mostly about nothing but headin' home to supper."

"So we'll want to be clearin' out of here before long then, won't we?"

Ike scowled. "You're right. It's time and past time."

"But first," Lolena said, "you might as well go ahead and get it over with."

"Get what over with?"

Lolena hesitated, listening to the rhythmic thumping sound and the stifled whimpers coming from one of the upstairs rooms. Jabbing a thumb toward the ceiling, she said, "That. The very thing you been sittin' there stewin' about … takin' your own self a turn with one or both of those farm fresh dollies."

Ike's scowl took on a suspicious slant. "Are you serious? You'd allow me that?"

"Hell, you're a rut-hungry man, ain't you? What else would I expect?"

A corner of Ike's mouth twitched. "I can't deny havin' me a healthy hunger when it comes to ruttin'. Reckon you know that as well as anybody. Considerin' that, what goes on between you and me I mean, I can't help wonderin'—"

"Aw, knock it off. You think I think this thing between us is headed down a primrose path with weddin' bells ringin' in the background or something? We happen to be warmin' the same bedroll for the time being 'cause it's handy for us and we both know a bullet with our name on it could be around the next corner. That's all. And don't forget those past times you and me got to chappin' each other's ass and I took up with Owen for a while." Lolena shrugged nonchalantly. "So, out of the blue, you got a crack at something new and fresh. Should I be so narrow-minded as to stand in the way of you havin' a little side diddle?"

Ike chuckled with increasing delight. "Goddamn, gal, you are something special!"

Lolena emitted her own chuckle, giving it a decidedly lewd twist. "You just make sure you remember that, in case I get a hankerin' and the chance for a side diddle of my own. Recall how I mentioned that knife-wieldin' Frenchy of ours a little while back? I might've only been kiddin' then but, a little while ago, when he went chasin' the daughter outside, I got me a peek at his free-swingin' tallywacker and, wow, I gotta tell you—"

"Don't go pushin' things too far. I may not be as charitable-minded as you," Ike warned her. "For your part, though, are you really serious about not carin' if I have me a poke with those rancher gals?"

"Go ahead," Lolena sighed. "You won't be no good tryin' to rob a bank all hump-backed like a randy alley cat anyway. Just get it the hell over with. And tell those other hose-swingers to finish up, too, so we can get about our business. We're *supposed* to be bank robbers, in case everybody forgot."

Ike stood up, smiling again. "By God, darlin', you *are* something special. And don't think I don't ..." He let his words trail off and the smile faltered. Canting his head to one side, he leaned his body that same way and peered intently out through the room's curtained windows.

"What is it?" Lolena wanted to know.

"Something's burning. I smell smoke. Don't you?"

Lolena rose too, as Ike moved to the window in long strides.

At the window, Ike yanked the curtains open wide and peered out even more intently, eyes raking everything in his field of vision. Lolena moved up behind him, a meaty hand coming to rest on the grips of the six-shooter in the holster of the gun belt cinched around the waist of her bib overalls.

Ike's body suddenly went rigid and he snapped out a curse. "Sonofabitch! That lean-to shelter out there behind the corral is afire. See it? Those penned up remuda horses are already circling in a panic—if they bust out and break into a stampede, they'll likely sweep our horses along with 'em. Then we'll be in a fine howdy-do!"

"I'll make for our horses and try to keep 'em under control," said Lolena, turning and starting for a side door that exited to the outside, where the gang's mounts were tied to a hitch rail. "You round up the rest of the men and tell 'em to pull out their peckers and get their asses in gear—if this ain't a sure sign it's time for us to hightail outta here, then I don't know what is … And don't forget to bring those sacks of supplies with you when you come!"

"Those goddamn morons!" Ike roared. "I told 'em to make sure one stayed on lookout while the others was diddlin'. They should have spotted that fire way before I did."

He pulled the long-barreled Schofield from his belt, aimed it toward the ceiling, and began squeezing off rounds as he bellowed, "Come a-runnin'! Come a-runnin', you assholes, and be quick about it."

* * *

Lolena emerged from the house and hurried toward the horses at the hitch rail. Before she reached them, however, she was stopped short by a voice calling out sharply from behind some nearby tall bushes.

"Hold it right there, Lolena! Don't go any closer to the horses, and don't let your hand drop any closer to that gun on your hip."

Lolena did as she'd been told, standing still, breathing heavily as she cranked her head around to try and get a look at who was behind the disembodied voice. What she saw was Earnest Tell step into sight, holding a Henry repeating rifle trained on her. He moved smoothly, seeming almost to glide, and was careful to always keep the tall bush between him and the house.

"You," Lolena said tightly. "You're that deputy from Emmett. The one who tried to keep my man Ike behind bars."

"That'd be me," Tell agreed. "And I full intend to see him behind bars again … or dead, if that's the way he wants it."

"Comes to that, you might be the one who dies tryin'."

"Could be. But I wouldn't count on it. Now walk on

over here to me. Slow and easy, and keep those hands wide and clear."

Once again Lolena did as she was told. As she moved toward him, she said, "What are you gonna to do to me?"

"Save your life, maybe. I'm gonna slap some handcuffs on you and shove you out of the way so you'll be safe from what comes next."

"What's gonna come next," Lolena said, turning her back to Tell as he shook out a set of cuffs, jerked her wrists together, and clamped on the bracelets, "is my boys bargin' out here any second and fillin' your black ass so full of lead you'll hit the dirt like a boat anchor."

Tell smiled as the big woman cranked her head around once again to glare at him. "That might be the case," he said, "if they don't get distracted by something else."

"What the hell's that supposed to mean? Distracted by what?"

"Oh," said Tell, blinking innocently. "Did I forget to mention that me and my partner borrowed a couple sticks of dynamite out of your saddlebags?"

Lolena looked dumbfounded for a long moment, her mouth hanging open like a fish out of water. Before she could clap it shut in order to say anything further, the long, low-roofed lean-to structure on the back side of the remuda corral exploded to hell and gone, sending a boiling cloud of smoke and dust high into the air and spewing a downpour of splinters and ragged slabs of wood.

* * *

Inside the house, Owen, Mapes, and Despare had just come half-scrambling, half-stumbling down the stairs in response to Ike's gunfire-laced summons. They swarmed into the dining room, still stomping back into their boots and pulling on articles of partially discarded clothing. All three were scowling and bleary-eyed but each had taken time to buckle on his gun belt and was brandishing a drawn pistol.

"What the hell's all the commotion?" Owen wanted to know.

"I'll tell you what all the commotion is," Ike snarled. "While you dick-brained idiots were—" That's all he got out before the explosion went off.

The whole house trembled from the concussion. Windows rattled, puffs of dust and plaster drifted down from the ceiling, and fine china on display along one wall of the dining room wobbled, some pieces toppling and shattering. The four men hunched their shoulders and ducked their heads out of reflex, as if in fear the house was going to collapse on them.

Straightening up from that involuntary response, Ike once again ran to the window out of which he could see the corral where he'd spotted the fire. He now saw a huge cloud of smoke and dust billowing skyward from where the lean-to had stood the last time he looked. And he saw and heard something else. He saw the fear-crazed remuda herd surge against the fence rails of the corral and break free, immediately picking up momentum and flowing into a full tilt stampede. The pounding of their hooves quickly grew in volume so that the sound became like a drawn-out extension of the explosion's rumble. Ike realized that, exactly like he'd been worried about, the path the fleeing nags were taking would brush them very close to the side of the house where the gang's mounts were hitch-railed.

But then, before he could react to a concern that was now becoming a certainty, Ike saw something more that froze him in place. Riding behind the wall of stamped-ing animals, reverse-melting out of the cloud of smoke and dust and tongues of flames now starting to lick up out of the lean-to ruins, came a horseman leaned forward in his saddle and charging hard.

"Who's that sonofabitch?" asked Owen crowding in beside his brother.

"How the hell should I know? But what I do know is that he's gonna to be a *dead* sonofabitch in about half a minute."

Ike jerked away from the window and wheeled around. He started snapping off orders, shouting to be heard over the low roar of the approaching stampede. "Owen, you take Mapes and get on out that side door to where we left our horses hitched to the rail out there—help Lolena keep a tight hold on 'em so's they don't get swept away in that stampede … Despare, you come out the front with me. We're gonna confront whoever that dynamitin' sonofabitch out there is and, by the time we're done with him, his brisket is apt to be exploded right out what's left of his interferin' ass!"

* * *

The Lawyer spurred Redemption hard, pushing the Morgan up close behind the stampeding remuda herd. His plan all along was to veer off and aim straight for the house when he got in closer. The sight of two men coming out the front door brandishing guns did nothing to change his mind. In fact, recognizing one of them to be the hated Jules Despare only added intensity to his focus. Knowing he was partially obscured by the boiling dust being kicked up by the stampede, The Lawyer's main concern then became finding a way to make certain Despare knew who he was before he killed the murderous piece of slime.

* * *

As the stampede thundered in their direction, Tell gripped the hefty Lolena by her shoulders and shoved her tight against the trunk of a young cottonwood tree growing up out of the stand of tall bushes. "Stay here, you'll be safe," he told her, speaking close to her ear in order to be heard above the din of the approaching hoofbeats. Then he pushed away and turned toward the house's side door, knowing that—as pre-arranged—by this time The Lawyer would be closing in on the front.

The ex-deputy had scarcely taken a step, however, when the door ahead of him burst open and Owen and Mapes came scrambling out, eyes wild above drawn pistols. Spotting Tell directly in their path, Owen jerked to a halt. Crowded close behind him, Mapes kept coming and slammed against the younger Selkirk. The collision caused both men to stagger and struggle for an awkward moment to maintain their balance in the doorway.

This second of imbalance and confusion gave Tell an advantage over the situation, despite the two guns being brandished against him. He still clutched his Henry repeater. Without hesitation, he dropped into a slight crouch and aimed from the hip. Any nonsense like calling for killers like these to throw down their weapons and surrender peacefully would only have gotten a bellyful of lead by way of a response. So Tell beat them to the punch with two rapid-fire rounds from the Henry.

Both slugs tore into Owen. One punched in a half inch under the tip of his sternum. The other hit about three inches off to the right, ripping through his rib cage and exiting under his shoulder blade before punching into Mapes's belly.

Owen merely emitted two soft grunts that sounded like "Ugh!" "Ugh!" as his knees slowly buckled and the gun slipped from his dying fingers.

Mapes's belly wound, on the other hand, brought forth enough wailing and cussing for half a dozen men. He thrashed back and forth like a wild thing, banging first against one side of the doorway and then the other as Owen sank down in front of him. But, in the midst of this, Mapes managed to get off a single frantic shot that sizzled out and blasted a chunk of bloody meat out the side of Tell's right thigh. Through the fiery pain streaking from his leg up through his torso, Tell stayed focus enough to raise the Henry and return fire, this time a more carefully aimed shot. The slug entered Mapes's left eye and took off most of that side of his face as the impact sent him hurtling backward.

Tell lurched a half step to one side but then re-steadied himself, keeping the Henry raised and ready in case all the fight wasn't out of the pair he'd just put down. The combination of his concentration on this and the ground-jarring rumble as the stampede raked around the end of the house and came streaming past only a few yards away, made Tell completely oblivious to the specter of Lolena coming up on his rear. She was building up a head of steam, running in her ponderous manner made even more so by the fact of having her arms still cuffed behind her back. At the last second, she tucked her head down and rammed it square between the ex-deputy's shoulder blades.

Tell was caught off guard by the blow that struck with the force of a whooshing roundhouse punch. His head snapped back and he heard his spine crack, his body bowing in the wrong direction even as he staggered a step forward.

Lolena herself was also momentarily stunned by the impact, but quickly shook it off—literally shaking her head from side to side like an enraged bull. "Murderin' black sonofabitch!" she hollered. And then, before Tell could get turned to face her, she kicked out viciously and drove the toe of her heavy boot into the gaping, bleeding hole that Mapes's bullet had torn out of his thigh.

The ex-deputy screamed in agony. But, at the same time, the pain and the threat of what this crazed woman might do next spurred something inside of him, driving him past the pain and reminding him of the vengeance he had sworn to deliver. Turning the agonized sound coming out of his throat into a war cry, Tell wheeled about and lunged to meet Lolena when she came at him again. He drove the butt of the Henry straight into her solar plexus, stopping her short and forcing a great gush of air out of her massive lungs. Lolena gnashed her teeth and spittle foamed at the corners of her mouth as she tried to force out some more cuss words. Twisting around further, Tell drew back with the Henry and then uncoiled hard and fast, this time slashing the butt of the rifle across the heavy cheek bone on the side of Lolena's broad face.

The woman pitched away without making a sound. Her upper body was turned part way around by the force of the blow and it sent her stumbling, leaning forward now, pulled off balance. When her toe caught on a clump of dirt, it threw her even more off balance and suddenly she had staggered out into the path of the horses on the edge of the stampede. A big roan stallion knocked her down and as she fell a terrified bleat of sound escaped her before the hooves of the roan and then those of a half dozen more horses coming behind him trampled her into a lifeless lump soon lost from sight in the swirling dust.

* * *

Making his break from behind the stampede, The Lawyer urged Redemption over close to a covered well that had been put in place not far from the front of the house. Slowing the Morgan just enough, he sprang fluidly from the saddle and went into a rolling tumble that brought him up behind the cover of the adobe bricks that encircled the well. At the same time, this allowed Redemption to gallop on out of the line of fire—which came mere seconds later when Ike and Despare began pouring lead at The Lawyer. The slugs smacked harmlessly into the thick adobe and made sharp *thwack!* sounds as they took bites out of the weathered wooden uprights that supported the peaked roof above the well.

Thick clouds of yellowish dust continued to roll in the wake of the stampeding horses and for a time it effectively blurred sight between The Lawyer's position and the men in front of the house. The Lawyer was counting on this. He let Ike and Despare waste their angry, frantic volley and then, in the lull where he calculated they would be reloading and while the dust screen was still at its thickest, he rose up and came out from behind the well.

In long, purposeful strides, The Lawyer began walking straight for the house. He held the Remington at arm's length, aiming carefully as the layers of dust thinned, and started squeezing off rounds.

Due to Ike's reputation as a gunman—in contrast to Despare, who was better known for knife work—The Lawyer concentrated first on the gang leader, meaning to try and eliminate him as a threat as soon as possible. Succeeding in this came quicker and easier than he'd dared hope. Three of The Lawyer's bullets found Ike as true as if they had eyes. Before the older Selkirk brother ever got off another shot, he took slugs to the shoulder, collar bone, and heart, slamming him back against the house and leaving him to slide slowly down, dying, in a bright smear of blood.

The Lawyer continued on through the ever-thinning layers of dust. He swung his attention to Despare, who had begun throwing return fire but in a half-furtive manner, especially as he saw Ike go down. Abruptly, after slugs from The Lawyer had knocked off his hat and grazed the side of his neck, the Frenchman flung his pistol to the ground and raised his hands. Truthfully, he'd lost count of exactly how many shots The Lawyer had fired. He might have only one or two live rounds left. Or none. But Despare wasn't willing to take that risk.

"No! That's enough for me. Don't shoot no more," he wailed.

The Lawyer kept striding closer, his expression set in ice, his pistol centered on Despare's chest. "But it's not enough for me," he said in a raspy voice, barely above a whisper.

"Wh–what do you mean?" Despare stammered. "It's over … I surrender."

The Lawyer came to a halt directly in front of the cowering man. "Surrender's not an option … not for you."

A flood of emotions poured rapidly through the Frenchman's eyes … confusion, fear, panic, anger … and then desperation. It was the latter that locked in place and out of it came a desperate act. One of the hands Despare held raised above his shoulders suddenly flashed down behind the back of his neck, reaching inside his shirt collar, and came out with a menacing Bowie knife that he swung in a slashing motion aimed at The Lawyer's throat.

The Lawyer pulled back reflexively, unable to avoid the point of the knife altogether but succeeding in keeping it from sinking deep enough to cause serious damage. Still, it left a long, stinging track under his Adam's apple that immediately began oozing blood and was enough to cause him to jerk his gun hand off to one side and inadvertently pull the trigger. The Remington harmlessly discharged its sixth and final bullet—the count being clear in The Lawyer's mind, even if it wasn't to Despare. Recognizing this, The Lawyer used the gun to strike a clubbing blow to the side of Despare's head and then discarded the Remington altogether and instead clamped a double grip on the wrist of the Frenchman's knife hand.

Both men toppled to the ground. Rolling in the dirt and their own blood, they struggled for control of the knife. Gradually, relentlessly, The Lawyer was able to get the blade turned until he had the point pricking through the cloth of Despare's shirt and into the flesh over his heart.

Once again the Frenchman's eyes swam with frantic emotions as he gazed up at the face of the man who was about to kill him. "You!" he suddenly gasped. "You're The Lawyer."

"That's what some call me," The Lawyer responded, his words coming between rapid, ragged breaths. "But to you, you sonofabitch, I'm more than that … I'm judge … jury … and executioner!"

And then, summoning a burst of enraged strength,

he threw the full weight of his body over the grip he had on Despare's own knife and drove all ten inches of the blade deep into the squirming black thing that passed for the butcher's heart.

EPILOGUE

The Lawyer came out of the house and sat down wearily on the ledge of the front porch, next to where Tell was already seated. The bodies of Ike and Despare lay to either side, still where they had fallen.

Tell stopped messing with the bandage that had been rather hastily knotted over his wounded thigh and looked up at The Lawyer. "The women okay?"

"They're alive," The Lawyer answered distantly. "How 'okay' they are after what they've been through … it will take a while to know that."

"For their sake, let's hope when Thornberry sends some folks out from town they think to bring the doctor along with 'em."

The Lawyer gestured toward Tell's most recent bandage. "For your sake, too. The thigh *and* the beating you took earlier."

"What about you?" Tell replied, gesturing in turn to the neckerchief tied over the knife gash on The Lawyer's throat.

"That's just a scratch. I've gotten worse nicks from shaving."

"Yeah. Right."

Both men were quiet for a long minute. The only sound was the muted crackle of the flames licking at the remains of the corral lean-to that had caught fire after the explosion.

"Before any townsfolk arrive, the smoke from that fire'll probably draw the attention of some of the men out brandin' cattle," Tell opined. "Gonna be a helluva shock for 'em when they show up."

"Bound to be."

Tell let another stretch of silence go by before he said, "What we did here … Was it justice? Or just vengeance?"

"Whatever you call it, it was the right thing. We did what we had to, they got what they had coming."

"'According to deserts' … I remember that part from what you said earlier, when you were explaining how all those things—justice, vengeance, retribution—are sort of cut from the same cloth. But how most people only consider it justice when it comes with a legal ruling."

"But we're not most people, are we?" The Lawyer pointed out. "Tell you what … How about we split the difference and call it retribution. Can you live with that?"

Tell took his time considering. Then: "Yeah. Yeah, I can … I can live with that just fine."

†

ABOUT THE AUTHOR

 Wayne Dundee lives in the once-notorious old cowtown of Ogallala, on the hinge of Nebraska's panhandle. A widower, retired from a managerial position in the magnetics industry, Dundee now devotes full time to his writing.

To date, Dundee has had nearly a score of novels and novellas plus over thirty short stories published. Much of his work has featured his PI protagonist, Joe Hannibal (celebrating over thirty years on the fictional detective scene and appearing most recently in Blade of the Tiger, 2013). He also dabbles in fantasy and straight crime, and lately has done some notable work in the Western genre. His 2010 Western short story, "This Old Star," won a Peacemaker Award from the Western Fictioneers writers' organization. His 2011 novel Dismal River won a Peacemaker in the Best First Western Novel category. His 2012 story "Adeline" won a third Peacemaker, again in the short story category.

Titles in the Hannibal series have been translated into several languages and nominated for an Edgar, an Anthony, and six Shamus Awards. Dundee is also the founder and original editor of *Hardboiled Magazine*.

If you enjoyed reading The Lawyer's adventures, you might also like these Cash Laramie novellas by Wayne D. Dundee. Available from BEAT to a PULP books at www.beattoapulp.com.

ಹಿ೦೮

Cash Laramie makes his way down the side of a mountain with a prisoner in tow and two prostitutes eager to flee a mining town that's gone bust, looking to make a new life for themselves. An early winter storm promises to make the journey more than a normal struggle. And, leaving town with two of its most precious gems, the prostitutes, puts Cash in the crosshairs of an angry gang of men who are willing to keep the women in town ... at any cost.

U.S. Marshal Cash Laramie is sent out to locate a shipment of stolen guns in the Vedauwoo area of Wyoming where the rocky terrain is treacherous and enshrouded in mystical beauty. In his quest, Cash goes up against an amoral opportunist looking to stir up discord in the region by selling the weapons to a group of Native Americans.

It's been weeks since the famed "Outlaw Marshal" has been heard from. Meanwhile, at the Federal Marshal headquarters in Cheyenne, Wyoming, some disturbing reports are starting to filter in about the notorious Driscoll Gang rapidly hitting a series of banks, allegedly with the aid of a badge-wearing accomplice claiming to be Laramie. Can it be true? Can it be that the lawman with the hair-trigger temper and the mile-wide independent streak has finally gone completely rogue?

Other titles from BEAT to a PULP

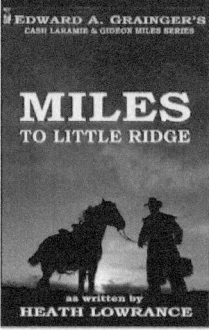
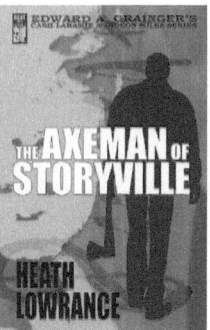

 BEAT to a PULP
PO Box 173
Freeville, New York 13068
USA
Email: btapzine@beattoapulp.com
Visit us at www.beattoapulp.com